A
LITTLE
FEAR

A LITTLE FEAR

Patricia Wrightson

A MARGARET K. MCELDERRY BOOK

ATHENEUM   NEW YORK   1983

LIBRARY OF CONGRESS CATALOGING IN PUBLICATION DATA
Wrightson, Patricia.
    A little fear.
    "A Margaret K. McElderry book."
    Summary: A strong-minded old woman struggles with
an ancient gnome for the right to live
in her own small cottage.
    I. Title.
PZ7.W9593Li   1983   [Fic]   83-2784
ISBN 0-689-50291-5

Copyright © 1983 by Patricia Wrightson
All rights reserved
Printed and bound by Fairfield Graphics
Fairfield, Pennsylvania
Designed by Christine Kettner
First American Edition

A
LITTLE
FEAR

1

Old Mrs Tucker sat in her room at Sunset House, a home for elder citizens, just as her anxious family had persuaded her to do. Her room was fresh and bright and neat and just like all the other rooms in Sunset House. There were off-white walls with one tidy peg to hang a picture, a mottled brown carpet, modern furniture that was easy to clean, and one deeply cushioned chair for rocking or reclining in comfort. There were only a few things of her own to make Mrs Tucker's room different from the others: the bright patchwork rug on her bed, knitted from scraps of wool of many colours; the old cup and saucer from her mother's set with the pink roses on them; the stern photograph of Harry, who had been her husband, hanging from the one peg; and Mrs Tucker herself.

Mrs Tucker was still almost six feet tall, with a large-boned frame that age and hard work had made gaunt. Her white hair made her look even taller: she insisted on wearing it twisted into an upside-down icecream-cone on top of her head, with little curly bits escaping round her face. She sat bolt upright on the very edge of the reclining chair, her bunioned feet in their oddly shaped slippers placed square on the mottled carpet. Her tiny white moustache was almost invisible, but it was bristling. Her eyes were an old, clear blue with no tinge of grey, and they were glinting.

'Helen!' snapped Mrs Tucker. 'I'm not childish yet. I won't be made a child.'

Her daughter Helen, who was plump and short and anxious, with hair already going grey, flushed and said, 'No, Mother, of course not.' Her granddaughter Valerie gazed at her with admiration. Mrs Tucker gazed back for a moment, then shifted her eyes and sighed impatiently.

When you were old, she knew, you really were a sort of child. When the things you used to do were all done, and your body and your mind grew slower, other people took over. They called you dear, or Agnes, just as if you were a child, and kept you in a clean bright nursery, and brought you warm underclothes that you didn't want. They worried and looked after you until, if you weren't careful, you were a prisoner of their care. Just like a child.

'It's my own fault,' muttered Mrs Tucker, and Helen smiled and laid the warm woollen undershirt on a chair. But Mrs Tucker certainly hadn't been thinking of the undershirt.

She knew that her mind was indeed slower now. It pushed the jigsaw pieces of thought this way and that; but it made a whole picture in the end. It was making one now, while Helen chattered about Valerie's school and the prices of things; Mrs Tucker nodded, pretending to listen. If your eyes were weak you wore glasses; if your teeth were gone you wore dentures; if your mind was slow you gave it more time.

'. . . gone up *five cents*!' cried Helen, and Mrs Tucker nodded.

'I remember when bread went up to sixpence a loaf. You'd just started school.'

And that was no stray jigsaw piece but part of the right picture. Bread sixpence a loaf and Helen starting school: they were on the farm. Milking, separating, scrubbing down in the dark of morning and night. Feeding calves and pigs and poultry, chopping wood. No electricity then; oil lamps and an old wood-burning stove, and a copper instead of a washing machine. No town water-supply, a rainwater tank and an old pump down at the creek. A good life, hard and lonely and free; doing for yourself, nobody's fussed-about child . . . Mrs Tucker's head drooped. Her eyes closed and she smiled a little.

Helen stopped talking and made a sign to Valerie. They stood up very quietly and crept to the door.

'Take that thing with you,' said Mrs Tucker. 'You know I don't wear wool near my skin, never mind that it's midsummer.'

Helen hurried off, pretending not to hear, but Valerie ran back to take up the undershirt and to hug her grandmother and be prickled by the little white moustache.

'You're going to run away, aren't you?' she whispered, one child to another.

Mrs Tucker was outraged. 'Run away – rubbish! What's the child thinking of? Never run away in my life and I won't start now. I'd be a fool. Setting the family by the ears, getting mixed up with the police – what for?'

'Good luck anyway,' said Valerie, and fled.

She left Mrs Tucker sitting upright on the edge of the reclining chair, making angry little spitting noises like *tchah* and *tchut*. She was so upset that she had to go through a whole series of jigsaw pieces again. By late afternoon she was able to decide that Valerie was only guessing; there were no clues.

Valerie had probably never even heard of her great-uncle John Bright. Even to Helen he must be a hazy figure. He had lived alone and out of touch, in that isolated cottage on a river in another State, for so long that none of the family would remember him at all. Certainly none of them knew he had died last year, leaving all his property to his sister Agnes Tucker.

She thanked her stars that her mail was still her own; so far no one had thought of going through that to sort out the worrying things and save her from trouble. She was glad that her shyness and dislike of Sunset House had made her so secretive from the very beginning – that she'd zipped all the solicitor's letters into the deepest pocket of her large handbag, and smuggled her replies into the mailbox on the corner by waylaying kindly visitors or taking a short stroll. There were no clues; there was not even going to be a search.

Run away! Trust a child to think of that! Dragging her own heavy suitcase, she supposed, and leaving her dear old rug behind. Hobbling over the hard pavements on her bunions looking for a taxi – waiting nervously at the railway station for a vacant seat. No, no, no. Sunset House, or Helen herself, could look after all that and send her off in comfort, properly booked. And once on the train she could manage to change the booking for herself. People were always anxious to look after an old lady; it was just a question of getting them to do it in the way you and not they had chosen.

She had not smuggled out her letter to her old friend

Doris, who lived two States away. That had gone through the Sunset House office in the ordinary way. Soon she would begin to arrange her little visit to Doris. And, since she wasn't supposed to be a prisoner, no one could stop her.

'They needn't try,' she told Harry's photograph, shaking her head. 'And when I've found the cottage I can send them a letter through Doris. Just to say I'm stopping and they needn't worry.'

She was suddenly shaken with terror at the thought of leaving Sunset House and all its careful provisions for coping with the outside world; of exchanging it for some lonely old cottage on a river. She had to shut her eyes and remind herself about living at her own pace in her own kind of home, with a bit of garden to keep her going.

'I'm as strong as a horse,' she declared to Harry. 'If John could live there till he was eighty-five, so can I.' And she reminded herself again, with the cunning of the aged child, that people were always anxious to look after an old lady.

After that she dozed in her chair, telling over all the encouraging things she had learnt from the solicitor about her new home. Above flood level ... with a telephone ... electricity ... a refrigerator ... a school bus passing the end of the track ....

It would have been luxury on the farm.

2 ❧

The cottage stood empty and rusty-roofed on the nose of a ridge above swamp-flats. Pine and stringybark and wattle stood round it and led away up the ridge to ragged forest behind. On each side, wide-mouthed gullies rose to other ridges that carried the same ragged forest. This was country that had been cleared and farmed and deserted, where the forest was now struggling back.

In front, the cottage looked over she-oaks and tea-trees fringing the flat, to a drowned valley where the river widened into miles of water. The farther shore, blue-hazed and blotched with the smoke of cane-fires, was too distant for any other house to be seen. If there were others on this shore they were hidden by ridges and trees. Everything lay under the hard heat of January; the cottage stood small and alone and waited for fire.

It was very still and silent. Shadows lay black and still; muddy water lapped under tree-roots. Honey-eaters called but stayed hidden in shady treetops; a distant truck changed gear and a trawler worked somewhere on the river – these sounds only added tension to the spun-glass silence. The pelicans drawn up in lines on a shady bank were the only life to be seen. Yet life was swarming.

The glassy silence was spun from the shrilling of cicadas. Above the ground and under it swarmed millions of busy ants. In the shadows a dead branch flickered into life: a lace-wing was swallowed by a bearded dragon lizard. Where the water lapped, a terrified prawn broke through and skittered upright on its tail to escape from the swirl of an eel. Within the broken-down fence of the cottage a lemon tree was thick with aphis, and busy, purposeful ants ran up and down tending them; little flies swarmed round the last of the peach tree's crop; a cassia, delicately green with showers of golden blossom, was being stripped by a crowd of caterpillars as delicately green as the leaves. Jaws munched steadily, heads lifted only to grope for a new leaf. One caterpillar belched uncomfortably: skin-changing time again. But this time it found it had attached itself to the underside of a leaf; irritated, it began to harden into a pearly-green stocking.

In the mouth of an old well, the mud of a reed-choked dam, and the damper parts of the flat, frogs burrowed deeper into coolness. One of them had foolishly chosen the overflow-pipe of the cottage's rainwater tank; it squarked anxiously as the sun heated the iron pipe. The last pair of little sooty rats crept out of a wall of the cottage into the cooler shade underneath. When the great hot sun dipped down beyond the water, lighting it to red and gold, they scurried off through tunnels of grass to nest among fallen branches in the gully.

From its own camp a Njimbin watched them go and frowned. It was a gnome, a small spirit that had lived among these ridges while the forests grew and fell and the men came and went. Once it had hunted like the old

11

people but on its smaller scale – for the fierce bandicoot, the cunning swamp-rat, the swift lizard. It had robbed nests, trapped small birds and fish, dug out fat witchetty-grubs, chopped dark-brown pods of honey out of hollow trees. Now everything had changed. The Njimbin mourned over the change like a man – and made use of it like a man.

It grumbled over the white man's hives of big, dangerous bees but left the little native ones alone; it was easier now to chew sugar cane, or steal peaches and watermelons, than to chop out honey. It was easier to take fish from a trawler's net than to take them from the river. And when the land was cleared and the fences built, when the houses gave a new sort of shelter and shade, the Njimbin learnt new lessons in providing meat.

There was no need to hunt cunningly for rats when the shelter of the houses drew them near. It was easier to be a friend to rats – to draw water for them from taps into rusty cans, to remove the lids of feed-bins, to spring traps and warn of danger, to become a Clever Man among rats – and now and then to choose a good, fat, well-furred one and club it quietly with a waddy. The rats had become the Njimbin's stock; and if they knew it, they too found the new life easier.

But you couldn't hold rats with fences, and in the hardest part of summer the Njimbin was often short of meat. It called after the last two scurrying down to the gully, in the silent way it spoke to all those who were not spirits or men: 'Watch out, you! Snakes are hungry down there.'

'Rats are baking up here,' called one of the two slipping away.

The Njimbin remembered the frog baking in the overflow-pipe. It longed for storms, for gullies running and swamps squelching and the old dam filled. But only a few clouds came up from the west and drifted away north; it was not yet time for storms to ripen.

3 ❧

It was February when Mrs Tucker left Sunset House, carefully arranged in a taxi by the matron and with Helen to see her off on the train. She enjoyed the journey; all her plans worked, and excitement made her blue eyes brighter and her bony figure taller and straighter. A railway porter and a taxi driver took some trouble to arrange the last stage of her journey on a country bus. She reached the little town five miles from her cottage and stayed there for two days, making all the arrangements that she knew were needed in order to live alone in the country.

The appearance of a very tall and bony old lady with a screw of white hair on top, who intended to live by herself out at John Bright's place, surprised the people of the town. They set about looking after her as best they could. She would need meat and bread and groceries delivered to the cottage; they approved her plan to use the school bus but added a twelve-year-old passenger, young Ivan, who would bring the goods the rest of the way along her track for two dollars a week. She knew you couldn't live in the bush without gumboots: they sent her to the right shop, where a stout, kind assistant found boots that slipped easily over her bunions.

She sat in the solicitor's office for a long time, signed all the papers he gave her, allowed him to make helpful arrangements about money, and listened to more details about her property.

'A boat too? My stars! Oars or an outboard? I don't know outboards, but I used to be able to pull a pair of oars.'

The solicitor said there were oars. But he looked a little surprised and added that he had thought she might like to sell the boat; it should bring a couple of hundred.

'I'll keep it for now, any road,' said Mrs Tucker, her old eyes shining. 'If I can only pull six strokes – well, it'll be a change.'

The solicitor spoke warningly of mud and shallows and weeds; and then of isolation and loneliness, and the need for company. Mrs Tucker's moustache stiffened.

'I know the country; lived in it all my life. I'll have company.' And this was true, for hadn't she already found the dog?

Of course she knew that you couldn't live in the country without a dog. The local taxi driver, who knew it too, had found one for her in the pound. It was not, perhaps, a kind of dog very common in the country; the pound-keeper thought some tourist had dropped it on the way through.

'They'll be back to claim him, won't they?' Mrs Tucker suggested. The pound-keeper looked wooden.

'Never knew it happen yet. And who's going to drive out of his way to claim *that*?'

The dog was probably part beagle; the rest no one could have guessed. He had a beagle's drooping ears and appealing brown eyes, a long body and deep chest on very short legs, and a graceful plumed tail. His head and ears were black, his coat a rich, shining white inlaid here and there with shorter-haired patches of black. He seemed sadly aware that he was odd and that nobody loved an odd dog; but he appeared to face an unfriendly world with anxious dignity and Mrs Tucker liked the look of him. She thought he might be honest, caring, and not yet too abject.

'I'll claim him,' she said. She gave the dog a biscuit and a friendly whack on the shoulder, and went off with the taxi driver to buy a large basket. The dog gazed after her, wistful but not hopeful.

When at last she was driven by tourist roads and a rutted track to her cottage on the ridge, the dog sat in his basket on the back seat of the taxi and waited for whatever fate might bring. Surrounded by the packages and parcels that Mrs Tucker had bought to equip an empty house, himself just another of these provisions, he refused to sniff or explore and kept himself to himself.

It was an exciting moment when they topped one ridge and saw the cottage standing on the next. The taxi driver said later that he felt like Father Christmas; the old girl was so happy she couldn't sit still. Mrs Tucker would not have minded that; it made the driver good-humoured about carrying all her goods to the cottage, unlocking the back door, turning the power on at the main and starting the refrigerator. Still, she was glad when he had been paid and thanked and had driven away over the ridge. It meant that at last she could explore.

The cottage was very simple and rather ugly: four square rooms opening into each other, with verandahs at the front and back. The back one, looking east up the ridge, had been made into a bathroom and laundry with a little porch in between. The front verandah looked over the river-drowned valley that the local people called the Broad. All the windows and doors of the cottage, front to back and side to side, were placed in line so that winds and views could flow straight through. The verandahs and all the windows were screened with wire gauze. Mrs Tucker thought it very practical.

The two front rooms were empty except for some old furniture and stored newspapers and things of that kind. The back two, a kitchen and a bedroom, were properly furnished and full of John Bright's things: his saucepans and china and linen in the cupboards, his sweater behind the bedroom door, his shirts and overalls in a drawer. He had lived in these back rooms; they had been comfort and housework enough for him, and they would be for her too. Mrs Tucker unpacked some groceries, made tea, and sat down to drink it and think of John Bright.

'He was a good man,' she said to the dog who was sitting at her feet.

He beat his tail softly on the floor. As she walked through the house he had stayed at her heels, someone to talk to. He listened earnestly when she spoke, as if he wanted to understand, and always answered with a beat of the tail. Mrs Tucker now remembered that he needed a name; it was unfriendly without.

The only masculine names she could think of were Harry and John, either of which would have seemed ridiculous. Her mind, searching for other names, ridiculous. Her mind, searching for other names, rediscovered an old song that children had sung as they marched on bare feet into a two-roomed school:

> Some talk of Alexander
> And some of Hercules,
> Of Hector and Lysander . . .

An unhandy lot of names; you couldn't call a dog Hercules.

'Hector,' she said, considering. She decided that she didn't like it, and then that it was too late: the dog, listening earnestly, had responded at once as if he had been waiting for the name. And if he liked it, who else mattered?

'All right,' she said, giving in. 'Hector, then.'

They went outside into a heat heavy with the threat of storms, to inspect the yard inside the broken-down fence. Hector stayed at Mrs Tucker's heels but lifted his nose delicately, or buried it in the grass, to sample the smells of the place. The peach tree, standing amid the ruins of its crop, was in full leaf; the sooty lemon was scented with blossom and a locquat was rusty with buds. Mrs Tucker's mind played with jigsaw pieces: sprays for smut and sugar for jam.

She saw the cassia, whole branches now stripped to skeleton leaf-veins. Dozens of little translucent-green stockings hung from it; and while she looked a wave of butterflies, lime and lemon, came washing and tumbling round the corner of the cottage and broke over the tree. Mrs Tucker shook her head.

'What can you do?' she asked Hector. 'It's one or the other – flying flowers or flowers on the tree.' Hector looked grave, and Mrs Tucker turned the question over. 'Which do we want? The tree or the butterflies?' She knew it would take some deciding.

A new generation of caterpillars, still working on the cassia, had no doubts: they wanted the tree. They could do without the butterflies – a lot of flittering strangers cluttering up the food supply with eggs.

Behind the cottage was a car-shed with no car, where John Bright had stored gardening things and tools. Mrs Tucker inspected it with delight, discovering nails and hammer, screws and screwdriver, washers, putty, a stepladder, wire-cutters . . . . She had always fancied herself as a user of tools and her fingers had begun to itch.

'I don't trust the washer in that bathroom tap,' she told Hector.

Hector gave an absent minded beat of the tail. He was concerned about a shadow that had blinked away out of the shed leaving no scent. Something bigger than a cat but with the same spine-tingling feel; and what sort of thing could have no scent? He had a responsibility to this revered and wonderful person who had given him a name. He followed her outside watching suspiciously from under shaggy eyebrows.

On the north side of the shed they found a rotary clothes-hoist which Mrs Tucker wound up and down. This produced panic among the ants nesting in its centre pole and brought angry spiders to glare out of the hollow cross-pipes. Mrs Tucker didn't notice. She had discovered, south of the shed, a square patch of overgrown, sun-browned weeds: a vegetable garden, waiting to be weeded and tidied up. Tomorrow, in the cool before the sun, would be time enough to look at that. And the tumbledown fowlyard farther up the ridge hadn't been used for a long time; it could wait. Now it was time to go in out of the heat; to spread her knitted patchwork rug on the bed, get off her bunions, and doze and think a bit.

From the fowlyard, the old eyes of the Njimbin watched her go: strong in spirit, peaceful in mind, slow in legs and stiff in back. The Njimbin knew old women. It also knew dogs: hunters too big for a Njimbin's spear and too close to man to be led or managed by a Njimbin. Alone they hunted only for food, and a Njimbin was no food. Fed by a man, a dog hunted for fun. In its long time on the ridges above the Broad, the Njimbin had come to know old women and dogs; but it lived only for now and never drew on the past to plan for the future. A sly and tricky spirit, quick to seize the chance of the moment, but not wise. It only watched, then climbed to the highest perch in the fowlhouse and squatted there to wait for the storm.

In the afternoon Mrs Tucker did a little unpacking while black clouds came bulging over the sky. In the evening it was still hot; thunder growled and lightning ripped the dusk. Great moths and beetles came beating and fumbling at the screens, trying to force a way in to light and shelter. Tiny things crept through the wire gauze and darted about the light-bulb. Then the wind came hurtling over the water to hump under the verandah roof and scream thinly through the wire gauze, and rain pounded on the iron roof and beat and splashed on the ground.

Hector withdrew under the kitchen table, flattened himself to the floor like a hunter's trophy-rug, and watched Mrs Tucker with misery and reproach from between his outspread ears. A spider as big as her hand appeared high on the kitchen wall. Tiny insects came tumbling from the light into her hair. The house trembled in the wind.

Mrs Tucker spoke bracingly to Hector. She aimed a spray-can at the spider, drove it into the dark front room and shut the door. She squirted the small insects and watched them drop flickering to the table, to be replaced by more. Then, since there was nothing else she could do, she went to bed in John's room with his sweater hanging on the door.

The Njimbin squatted on its perch in the fowlhouse and covered itself with a tattered rug of rat-fur while the rain poured through a gap in the roof. It listened closely to frog-bellows reverberating in downpipes and the echoing sound of water running into the tank. When the storm passed and the house was dark it ventured to light a tiny fire in a dry corner of the fowlhouse and to roast a lizard. While it ate the lizard it listened to the rhythmic grunting of a koala on the next ridge, the scuttle of a possum on the cottage roof, and the screams of fruit-bats in a nearby tree.

It thought that soon, if there were more storms and the gullies ran often enough, the rats might be persuaded to move back.

4 🍂

Mrs Tucker began work on the vegetable patch the next morning, before the sun climbed over the eastern ridge bringing the heat. She put on her gumboots, a pair of John's overalls and some old gloves from the shed, and knelt on the wet grass prodding among weeds with a little fork. She loosened the weeds, pulled out a few handfuls, and discovered several beheaded cabbage-stalks sprouting new yellowed leaves.

'Now that's a good thing,' she told Hector. 'They'll soon green up with the rain and the sun, and we might get a picking while new seeds are coming on.'

Hector was not listening. He was intent on the fresh scents in the rain-washed grass, making short, excited runs to and fro, sometimes delicately lifting his muzzle for a long and thoughtful tasting. He was a town dog, inexperienced. No night-time strayings of cats and dogs in town had prepared him for anything like this. The cottage had been besieged overnight. If he could believe his nose, the intruders had been furred and scaled and skinned; hopping, wriggling, running; eaters of leaves and insects and flesh. A shiver ran through him from

22

nose to tail and there was a spark in his sober eyes. Mrs Tucker smiled and climbed laboriously upright.

'That's enough for one day,' she said, taking off her gloves. 'No good rushing at it. We'll go and look for the boat.'

They went down the ridge and over the flats on a track that was damp but firm. Mrs Tucker went slowly, leaning on a bent stick of wattle she had found by the gate-post. Hector started off properly at heel but was led by his nose into widening circles. They walked through the rich gold splashes of buttercups and the soft blue of lobelia, found pale violets in shady places, disturbed sleeping butterflies clinging with folded wings to stems of grass. Hector nosed out a bearded-dragon lizard, sluggish with coolness and waiting for the sun to quicken it, only able to open its wide jaws and gape at him. At this Hector lost the last of his dignified control and barked wildly until Mrs Tucker called him off.

Through oaks and tea-trees they came suddenly to the edge of the Broad, with the high tide overflowing into the couch-grass and eroded roots of trees trampling it down. Hector took one horrified look and drooped. He quickly turned his back on the Broad and pretended to find a scent leading away to the tea-trees.

'*Oho!*' cried Mrs Tucker accusingly. 'Scared of the water – a great big dog like you!'

Hector didn't seem to hear.

The water stretched away almost to the horizon, only ruffled here and there by threads of current. A drift of mist lay over the water, and reflections were oddly broken and scattered; sunrise colours still out of sight behind the eastern ridge, a tree-lined bank too far away to see.

'Something like a mirage, that must be,' Mrs Tucker murmured. She leaned against an oak and brought a horde of mosquitoes tumbling out of it to sing fiercely about her head and shoulders. They followed as she hurried away, slapping at them.

'Enough's enough,' said Mrs Tucker. 'We'll find the boat tomorrow. Come out of that, Hector, you'll be bitten by a spider. The lizard's long gone.'

As they came back to the cottage the sun rose and the heat began. While it lasted Mrs Tucker stayed indoors. She did a little housework, began a letter to her old friend Doris, and rested and thought. In the afternoon another storm blew up, struck briefly and disappeared over the ridge leaving cooler air behind. Mrs Tucker went out to dig a few more weeds, and uncovered a trailing stem of tomato with one bunch of leaves and two ripening fruit. There were neat, round, juicy holes eaten in the fruit.

The air was busy with wasps, dragonflies and butterflies, and with blowing curtains of tiny midges here and there. Crickets chirped endlessly until Mrs Tucker thought her ears were singing. Hector found a frog, nosed it in the rear, leapt back in surprise as the frog leapt forward, advanced cautiously and nosed it again. So they progressed in leaps across the yard while Mrs Tucker laughed in a hearty bellow that would have surprised the staff of Sunset House.

The Njimbin watched scornfully from under the back step. It had been stealing pumpkin seeds from Mrs Tucker's vegetable box as a present for the rats. It hoped to persuade them soon to move higher out of the gully.

24

That night great cream-and-gold scarabs came bumbling at the screens and grumbling under the doors. Little stingless midges swarmed through the wire gauze and danced about the light and tumbled into Mrs Tucker's hair. She decided that she might as well be out as in, and took Hector to watch the moon running between clouds. But the night was alive and awake, and they were not wanted there except by the singing swarms of mosquitoes. Down at the river swans conversed like ladies at an afternoon tea. A fat spider had hung its web from the peach tree to the wall and Mrs Tucker only dodged it by inches. A bat flitted against the white wall of the shed; an owl rose from a post almost under Mrs Tucker's hand; Hector growled deep in his throat at something she couldn't see and placed himself firmly in front of her. They went indoors again and to bed.

The Njimbin came down from the clothes hoist where Hector's growling had driven it and hurried to the gully with its gift of pumpkin seed. The rats fell on the seeds with joy, stole them from each other, and whisked them off to hide in their nests.

'Plenty more soon,' said the Njimbin kindly. 'The old woman's making a garden.'

'Aha!' cried the young rats. 'A garden!'

But an old rat stared at the Njimbin with bright, cunning eyes and said, 'We heard the dog.'

The Njimbin snorted. 'Dog! That fancy-coloured beast doesn't know one end of a frog from the other.'

'He may learn,' said the old rat. 'We should give him a little time.'

The Njimbin shrugged. 'If you don't mind being flooded out. Two storms in two days. I can keep the dog off you, but even a Clever Man can't keep back the storms.'

The old rat twitched his tail. 'A few storms to fill out the berries and curl the young bracken, that's all. You worry too much, old friend.'

The Njimbin smiled widely and went away dissatisfied.

Early next morning Mrs Tucker dug out a few more weeds. She found half a dozen onions rotting in the ground and a few yellow, stunted plants of silver beet. Her pleasure in these finds was spoilt by the fact that the young cabbage-leaves had been nibbled and the two ripening tomatoes had wholly vanished. She had found some packets of seed in the shed, but it began to seem a waste of time to plant them. She gave up gardening and wandered about with Hector, looking at the trailing wires of the broken fence and hobbling up to inspect the old fowlyard. If the fence had been whole it would have kept out nothing but cattle. The fowlyard, on the other hand, had a sagging fence of netting . . . had even been netted over against hawks . . . and gardening tools could be stored in the fowlhouse. She remembered the hammer and nails and the little light stepladder in the shed. Her blue eyes brightened.

'Come on, Hector!' she called. 'Enough's enough. We'll go and find the boat.'

That morning they did find the boat. It was pulled far up on the bank of the Broad among trees, with its oars laid neatly under the seats. Hector had never seen a boat and jumped in to sniff and explore it, while Mrs Tucker explored it from outside. It was certainly hers, for her brother had painted her name across its stern – *Agnes*, in large uneven letters; and underneath, printed smaller, *J. Bright, Bright's Road, The Broad.*

That, she supposed, was in case it was lost in a flood. She was moved that John had named his boat for her, and wished that she could climb aboard and try it out at once. It was no good wishing; the boat was too far from the water and she could not launch it without help. She put aside the thought of the boat and spent the next few days working happily on the fowlrun.

She knew fowlruns and wire netting. The base of this netting was still buried in the ground as it should be. She had only to haul the wire upward, straightening out the sags and stretching it tight, anchor the stretched bit to its post with a few nails, and bend the nail-heads upward to hold it. There was no one to count the hammer-strokes and shake his head, or to frown if she used a drill to get the nail started. She could manage three posts in a morning and another couple at sunset; she dragged her ladder from one to the next, smiling as her mind went back to the farm.

The Njimbin retreated into the tall, broad, sharp-edged leaves of the blady-grass and sulked. The rats came stealing up through their tunnels in the grass to watch and tease.

'Lost your camp, then, friend?'

The Njimbin put on a wide smile. 'Wait, I'll have a yard full of melons and tomatoes and peas – I heard her tell the dog.'

'She'll be in and out like a nestful of ants. Found your club, has she?'

'Am I as brainless as a rat? She's found nothing.'

27

'Well,' said the rats, flicking their tails happily, 'let us know when you're looking for a new camp.' They rustled away softly through their tunnels of grass.

The Njimbin snorted. It had camped in the fowlhouse for only twenty years, but it would not be put out by one old woman. The fowlhouse was a good camp, with a water tap nearby: like the houses of people, but smaller and more comfortable.

Now the dog was nosing in the blady-grass. The Njimbin grunted angrily and scuttled up a stringybark. The dog had become a daily nuisance, hunting for fun in the long grass and bracken while the old woman worked. It destroyed the nests of bandicoots and got itself scratched; it snuffled at an echidna and got itself pricked; nothing stopped it. A fool of a dog, thought the Njimbin in disgust: it even threw itself into the air after birds, barking wildly. It hardly knew the difference between a lizard and a snake, but so far no snake had bitten it in spite of the Njimbin's urging. The snakes were too shy and the dog too noisy – but the Njimbin kept on hoping.

For while Mrs Tucker worked and smiled and thought about the farm, Hector had discovered the tunnels of the rats. He nosed his way along them through the forest of blades, following the rat-scent and destroying the tunnels as he went. At the rustle of a lizard or a rat he came leaping up through the grass to check on his direction, scurried to and fro and came leaping up somewhere else. The rats rebuilt a tunnel or two at night when they gathered food, but they grew more and more cautious about coming up the ridge.

Mrs Tucker would laugh her bellowing laugh when he came leaping up from the grass, or when he threw himself into the air after a bird. A magpie and a spur-winged plover had begun to tease him, swooping low and leading him off on a useless chase. Hector would grow infuriated and hurtle after them with noisy barks.

'You'll grow wings one day,' Mrs Tucker would shout. She found no need to call him off, for there seemed no chance that Hector would ever catch anything at all. He had no real temper, she thought, and would never make a watchdog; but he was good company and she liked having him.

Meanwhile she had finished the run; she had a garden patch safe from birds and all the furry creatures. Now there was only the fowlhouse itself – a hinge adrift and a sheet of iron out of place. And the perches: take them out to make more room? Or use them to hang tools and a hose? She went inside to rest and think about the perches.

She still hadn't decided on Monday afternoon when young Ivan brought her weekly groceries. He came, a round-faced, freckled boy of twelve, riding over the ridges on his brother's motorbike. Hector received him in suspicious silence, placing himself between the boy and Mrs Tucker and showing that he had his own ideas about watchdogs. Mrs Tucker was perched on her stepladder, tugging sheets of iron into place.

'Ha!' she cried in welcome. 'Just the boy I wanted to see!'

Young Ivan stared. Repairing fowlhouses hadn't been allowed for in his weekly two dollars, but with her up there on her skinny old legs . . . . It turned out that she didn't want help with the fowlhouse, only with getting her boat on the water. He turned silently and strode down to the river.

29

Clearly he knew where to find the boat. Mrs Tucker let him go and climbed down from the ladder to fetch his money. Hector stayed on guard, as silent as young Ivan, beside the unnecessary gate. Young Ivan returned, was paid and thanked, and rode away without having uttered a word.

'Right,' said Mrs Tucker to Hector, taking up her bent stick of wattle, 'we'll go and have a look.'

It was not Hector's favourite walk but he went dutifully, only hanging back among the tea-trees as usual. Young Ivan had left the boat tied to an oak and nose-in among its roots, at a point where there was a low bank rather than a muddy beach. It would probably be aground at low tide, but now it floated on a few inches of water in the gold-and-red dazzle of sunset.

Mrs Tucker untied the mooring line. She managed to climb aboard, sat down heavily, and began to fumble with the oars. 'Come on, Hector, if you're coming!' she called.

Hector took one look and froze: his revered and wonderful person was afloat on a vast expanse of water. He drooped and sagged. He crawled to the bank and lifted his muzzle and howled.

Mrs Tucker muttered *tchut* and *tchah* and pulled several strokes with the oars. Hector howled. Mrs Tucker let the boat drift a little and looked over the Broad at a line of pelicans, the hazy faraway shores, and the bank she had left which had grown dignified and mysterious with trees. Hector howled. The Njimbin, concealed among violets, scuttled up one of the oaks and cried silently to the pelicans, the eels, the lizards: 'See here! A dog with no belly! Scared of water!'

30

Mrs Tucker rowed about a little, brought the boat in and moored it again. She climbed out stiffly. 'We'll make a dog of you one day,' she told Hector, 'but not yet.'

Hector followed her home at a little distance and wearing his air of self-contained dignity.

The next morning Mrs Tucker finished the fowlhouse. Lying on her bed to rest and think, she made up her mind about the perches. In the afternoon she made several telephone calls. On the following morning she dressed in the sort of clothes that old ladies are expected to wear, dabbed a little powder on her moustache, and explained to Hector that she had some shopping to do and he must guard the place. Then she was driven away in the taxi.

Late in the afternoon she was driven home again, with such of her shopping as would fit into the taxi. There was no Hector waiting at the unnecessary gate; she thought he was chasing lizards in the blady-grass and was a little vexed that he did not come excitedly to welcome her. It took a little time to discover that he wasn't there at all.

Hector was gone.

5 🌿

When Mrs Tucker drove off in the taxi, leaving Hector alone for the first time, it seemed to him that the sad events of his earlier life were being repeated. First he pelted after the taxi on his short legs, yelping shrilly to remind Mrs Tucker that she had left him behind. As the taxi quickly vanished and the sound of its motor faded, he sat on the track, raised his muzzle and howled, throwing his voice far ahead, giving Mrs Tucker a last chance to remember him and come back. When even his ears could no longer hear anything at all, he sat drooping and dwindling like a candle in the fire.

After a time he dragged himself to his feet and slowly back up the ridge. At the cottage gate he collapsed, gazing hopelessly along the track to where it disappeared over the next ridge. He ate a little grass because he felt so unwell, flattened himself on the ground with his ears spread out, and went on staring hopelessly from between them. He expected to die there, faithfully on watch.

The spur-winged plover down on the flat jeered at him. It had a shrill, assertive scream that always made Hector leap after it in fury, but this time he only rolled his eyes towards it for a moment and gave a choked growl. An ant, laboriously toiling through the grass, mounted the tower of his nose. He snorted and shook it off.

From among the dark-green leathery leaves of the locquat tree the Njimbin watched in scorn. This was a dog – toothed and clawed to kill, with ears that caught the sound of the tide turning and a nose that twitched to the scent of a caterpillar. And there he lay, well-fed and miserable, mourning for the old woman. And when she returned, this miserable beast would rush about in pure delight and lay waste a nestful of rats for joy.

'Come!' called the Njimbin wordlessly to the plover on the flat; for the moment had brought its chance, and the dog was afraid of water, and the tide was high. The plover, always ready to tease, heard the call. It came sweeping up from the flat, swung low over Hector and screamed rudely.

Hector only stirred and growled. The plover beat a little way up the gully, circled and came back, swooped over Hector's head and screamed again. Hector gathered himself and rolled his eyes upward. They were lit with red. Even a bird could see that he was in no mood for teasing. But the plover was the worst kind of tease; signs of bad temper only spurred it on. It flew low and screamed again, and swept on over the ground, screaming as it went.

Hector roared in fury and hurled himself after it.

The plover turned down to the flat, yelling like an urchin. Hector went leaping and racing below it.

'The boat! The boat!' called the Njimbin, rushing ahead at a spirit's speed to untie the mooring line.

The plover circled and Hector plunged after it through mud. He was defending himself from an impudent attack. When the plover dived under she-oaks he hurtled after it, victory near. He only saw the river as a background – and the little boat, nosing among oak roots, seemed attached to the land as it had been on the day he jumped into it. The plover sat cheekily in the stern.

'Now,' whispered the Njimbin, low in the water by the boat. The plover shrieked, and Hector leapt for it, and the Njimbin shoved.

The plover was thrown off balance but beat its way into the air. Hector sat down hard in the boat, sprang up again to leap ashore, staggered as the boat rocked under him, and saw the river wickedly shining all around. He sat down again in the puddle of water that had collected in the boat and whined anxiously.

He heard water slap and suck against the boat, the chuckle of the Njimbin guiding it, and the wordless voice of the Njimbin low in the water.

'No good now,' said the Njimbin.

The boat turned into the current where the tide was beginning to run out. With the Njimbin pushing, it travelled a little faster than the tide. They went slowly down the drowned valley of the Broad towards its junction with the main river. Pelicans regarded them with solemn surprise.

'Scared of water,' the Njimbin explained. 'Half dead with fright. Never think he had teeth, would you?'

The pelicans drew off in their dignified way.

They passed the oak-fringed swamp-flats. The near bank grew steep, dark with tall pines and ironbark and old wattles. They shadowed the water that lay so still beyond the ruffle of the current. Great logs stood out of it, stranded by the last retreating flood and showing that the

34

river had not drowned the valley deep. Darters perched on the logs, looking down, and from out of the shadows a crowd of coots came wing-beating over the surface of the water with a sound like the crackle of fire in cane. Hector was startled and gave them a hunted look.

'Watch it!' called the Njimbin tauntingly. 'Poor dog's not used to it, you'll break his nerve.'

Above the tree-dark slope rose a green hill topped with a house. Hector stood up with a sudden lurch: even strange people were sometimes kind. He barked for help, but no one came out of the house to look.

'Empty,' said the Njimbin happily. 'No one there to hear.'

All the same it grew more careful, for it too knew that people will often rescue a dog or a drifting boat. It took the boat nearer the bank, where the trees screened it from the flood-free heights; and when it knew they were near some hidden cottage it fed Hector misleading information.

'Lonely country in there. All swamp, that.'

They rounded a point and joined the main river, a great sweep of water still nearly half a mile wide. Now there were houses in plain view on the near bank and the little town strung out along the far one, as well as trawlers and launches. The Njimbin took to the middle of the river and trusted to distance, for the current here was much faster and the boat still travelled ahead of it. From a distance it would be seen to be not drifting but under control, and the dog might look like a stooping man – if only he didn't howl. The Njimbin set out to distract him.

'I know a dog,' it said, looking teasingly over the stern, 'swims across here and back every day. Does it for fun.'

But Hector did not droop, as he had for shame before

the pelicans and coots. He stared ahead unmoved; he simply did not believe the Njimbin.

Ahead of them, absurdly frail and confident over the wide, strong water, a golden butterfly dipped and fluttered and rose.

'See that, now,' said the Njimbin, peeping over the stern again. 'No more than a couple of petals – if it lit on you you wouldn't feel it. But it's not scared of water.'

At last Hector was goaded into a grumbling reply. 'Flying – who wouldn't? Show me a butterfly swimming.'

The Njimbin was taken aback and had no answer ready. It covered this by calling to the butterfly instead. 'Ho, there! A good stand of wild cotton on the north bank near the turn!' For in these small ways it made itself a Clever Man among the creatures. The butterfly veered, recovered, and side-slipped into the breeze. Hector brooded darkly and the last of the town slid by.

Now the river opened wide among islands. There were islands with roads and towns and farms, islands of mangroves and mud, islands with one lonely house and a patch of bananas or cane. The Njimbin left the main river and took the boat on through channels and backwaters. Hector crept under the stern seat to escape from the sun.

Ancient paperbarks leaned over the water; the boat slid under their outflung branches. Mosquitoes came swarming out of them humming, and their humming sang upward to a whine as they found Hector under the seat. Dog! They swung and hovered over his shining fur, finding vulnerable places on paws and ears and belly. Hector came out from under the seat; he needed more room for scratching. Luckily the sun had now gone behind heavy, yellow-white clouds.

They crossed another channel and slid between mangroves. The boat slowed, tide-drifting: the Njimbin was calling to someone on the bank. 'Ho, old friend! So they keep you trapped on a muddy Island now.'

It was a Hairy Man, slouched in the fork of a mangrove tree and looking like a huge banksia-cone except for its pendant arms and squat legs. When Hector saw it he stiffened in spite of his hopeless situation, and the red glint came into his eyes: another of these things with no scent. In response to the Njimbin's call the Hairy Man only stared morosely; it had never regarded the Njimbin as a friend and had not even seen it for a century or so. But the Njimbin, pulling back on the drifting boat, seemed to feel very friendly.

'You want to look after yourself!' it shouted. 'Like me. See this dog here – no good, a pest, hunts the rats. I'm getting rid of it – gone for good when the tide turns. They won't trap me,' it boasted.

The Hairy Man stirred. 'No trap,' it said sullenly. 'I come and I go.'

'Ho,' said the Njimbin. 'No frogs here, though. You must be taking mud-crabs these days. Don't blame you; never did fancy frogs myself.'

It hauled itself out of the water to sit on the boat's stern and converse more easily. Hector saw it whole for the first time: a small man-thing with bushy white hair and beard and no scent; grey like stone and gnarled like an old root with age. Hector rose stiff-legged in the rocking boat, the hair raised along his spine and his shoulders hunched to spring. He growled deeply and juicily.

The Njimbin tumbled back over the stern and into the water. The Hairy Man livened up and broke into wheezy cackles.

'Can't trap *you*, eh? Near did, though, the pest of a dog. Near trapped you that time!'

For a moment the Njimbin seemed to snarl, but then it too was cackling. 'All bark and no bite, this feller,' it chortled, turning the joke against Hector. 'Wants to be quicker than that to catch a Njimbin, eh? Scared of water too, you know that?'

But the Hairy Man was morosely silent again and the boat was drifting past. The Njimbin called a last few words over its shoulder, its voice rising as the distance lengthened.

'You want frogs, you come out my way. I got a bit of swamp out there, I'll give you frogs! WE GOT SO MANY FROGS,' it shouted, 'WE KEEP STEPPING ON 'EM!' it roared. Then it lowered its voice again and muttered to itself. 'Frogs – silly old bundle. Give me a nice young rat, hand-fed and friendly, killed quick and roasted slow. That's the tucker. Frogs!'

Until mid-afternoon the Njimbin pushed and guided the boat seaward through the backwaters of the river. Hector growled a little, and dreamed of meeting the Njimbin on equal terms in some quiet back street; he lapped at the water that lay in the boat, and battled with mosquitoes. The current slowed, the boat grew heavier, the river lay smooth and languid under the clouds; and at last the Njimbin ran the boat into shallow water among spiky mangrove roots. It climbed with the mooring line into a tree and tied the boat to a low branch.

'Stop you drifting back on the tide,' it explained to

Hector from a safe distance. 'You'll be all right here; nothing but mud and water and a few crabs and lizards. A good life if you don't mind wet feet.' It dived, and Hector watched its white head bobbing away upriver.

The boat swung on the mooring line, its stern turning listlessly downstream. *Agnes*, it said; and *J. Bright, Bright's Road, The Broad*. But neither Hector nor the Njimbin could read.

Hector stared at the water; it stretched away into darkness among the mangroves with only a streak of mud showing here and there. He lifted his nose in short, testing sniffs: water and mud and dank things; no sun or grass, no people or furry things. Yet there were trees, and the boat was a hateful unsteady thing. He stood up, whined, ran a few steps to and fro, climbed on to a seat. He would have gone over the side and into the deep mud if the water had not stirred.

But there was a whisper somewhere; and a long, slow ripple came stealthily through the mangroves and slurped very softly around the boat. The boat grew uneasy and restless and Hector sat down. It tugged at its line, swinging its stern upriver. Hector wriggled and whined.

The tide had turned. It lapped among the mangroves and pulled and tugged at the boat. Hector broke into anxious yapping and then into a full-throated bark: nothing happened. Only the water deepened quickly.

Time went by and the cloudy afternoon darkened. Hector barked uselessly once or twice, and sometimes drank a little more of the water in the boat; it tasted like aspirin. A great, pale jellyfish came drifting silent and ghostly past the boat; and another, and another. A few

39

drops of rain fell into the water and sprang up from it again. A shower came up the river, hissing over the water and misting it. Hector was wet and cold. He lifted his muzzle and howled.

He howled softly at first; but as the rain fell and the tide rose and dinnertime approached, despair and misery came home to him. He lifted his voice to its full trumpet-strength and sang his sorrow to the sky.

He sang of treachery and loss and loneliness; of hunger and thirst and rain and mosquitoes; of the terror of dark water haunted by drifting white shapes. And when he had rested and drunk a little sour water he sang of them again. He sang to the sky, and to any sympathetic dog within reach of his powerful voice; and, though he didn't know it, to humans in lonely cottages on nearby islands. The rain had made a twilight early and long on the river, and Hector sang to it.

Hours went by and Hector howled; and his misery echoed in human ears, and human lips began to curse. And when those ears had endured all they could of Hector's misery and despair a cane-farmer came rowing out of the rain, and untied the mooring line, and towed Hector and *Agnes* away.

6

When the taxi had gone Mrs Tucker stood at the back
door, with three or four large packages dumped around
her on the porch floor, and shouted, 'Hector! Come out
of that!'

No Hector came rushing back from the blady-grass,
and she bristled indignantly. He mightn't be much of a
watchdog, but the least a dog could do was to welcome
his boss home with the proper signs of joy.

'I've no time to waste on you,' she called, and went
inside to change. She might just have time for a cup of tea
before the van brought the rest of her shopping. And that
would fetch young Hector back from his lizards, or Mrs
Tucker was a Dutchman.

She was pleased and excited about her shopping,
which solved the problem of the perches in a bold and
logical way. Once you thought of it there was no getting
away from it: you could use perches for a lot of things, but
what they were meant for was fowls. You could grow
vegetables in a fowlrun, or you could prop up an old bit
of wire netting in the back yard; and if you had the
fowlrun, why waste it? Fowls were more company than
vegetables. Mrs Tucker drank her tea quickly and hurried

outside. She had several things to do before the van arrived.

Bulging yellow-white clouds hid the sun and made it easier to work. She took one of the seed-boxes from the shed, lined it with grass, and put it in a corner of the fowlhouse for a nest. There was an old plant-trough under the workbench in the shed; she dragged it by stages to the fowlyard and filled it with water. She remembered that fowls were nervous and flighty in a strange place, and so she brought shellgrit and wheat from the packages in the porch to scatter in the fowlrun; it would give the poor things something to peck at and settle them down. She was so busy and excited that she hardly missed Hector at all.

The afternoon light faded early. A shower of rain was sweeping over the Broad when the van came labouring and clanking up the ridge. The fowls lay with their legs tied and their round yellow eyes goggling: one rooster and three hens, all white with lacy black collars. The van driver released them, and each in turn exploded out of his hands to run shrieking up and down the fowlyard.

When the van had left, Mrs Tucker put on John's old raincoat and stood watching the fowls with pleasure. She talked to them cheerfully, and made clucking noises, and threw them some more wheat. The rooster began to recover his poise, coaxing the hens with deep, throaty clucks to peck at the wheat. Mrs Tucker went happily inside; they were settling already.

It was only then that she recognized an uneasiness behind her pleasure: Hector had not come back. The long showery dusk kept her from going to look for him, but she called for some time from the back door and the front verandah.

'Hector! Here, boy. Hector! What's got into the dog?'

When his feeding time arrived she filled his dish and called again. He did not come, and she had to admit that he was lost. She knew, in fact, that it was worse than that, for a dog can't simply be lost from his own home. Hector was hurt – caught in a trap, pinned under a falling branch; or else someone had taken him away.

She spent a dreary, cheerless night, her old lace stern with worry. For once there were no insects beating at the gauze; raindrops, pelting like cannonballs, kept them away. Mrs Tucker sprayed a few spiders that came scuttling in under her doors, trod on a millepede or two that uncurled and hurried slowly away, and lay in bed listening to the bellowing chorus of frogs.

'Maggoty things,' she grumbled, for she had not expected so many frogs. All through the heat they had stayed hidden in their cool places, yellow eyes veiled and leather throats pumping, each one content to be alone. Storms had scarcely roused them; but now, with the showers sweeping over the ridges, the frogs remembered each other. From pipes and gutters and window-ledges, dams and wells and tanks, their voices beat like a chorus of muffled drums.

'Frog, frog, frog!' they called, seeking each other, and the chorus swelled until suddenly they stopped to listen. 'Come, come, come!' they boomed; and, 'Swamp, swamp, swamp!' Between choruses the rain whispered on the roof. They were lonely sounds, but Mrs Tucker had had a long day and they drugged her into sleep.

43

Once in the night something woke her; she thought it was the shrieking of fowls – maybe Hector had come home and startled them. She wrapped herself in the patchwork rug and went out to call him; but he didn't come, and after all she could hear nothing but frogs. She went back to bed.

The Njimbin had arrived some hours earlier, coming home on the high tide through the hissing and dancing of rain on the river. Like Mrs Tucker it had had a long day; it was cold and waterlogged, ready for a dry camp and a fire. But it was also full of swagger and self-satisfaction, and it first made its way up the gully to the nests of the rats.

The rats had been rebuilding because of the rain. The Njimbin found them nesting above ground-level in a great heap of dried branches and twigs where John Bright had once cleared a spread of wattle. The sooty little rats scampered along branches, chasing each other in games that were only half friendly; but when they saw the Njimbin they stilled, peering from among the twigs with bright, cautious eyes.

'Ho!' said the Njimbin. 'Washed out already, I see. I warned you. But you'll be all right now, I've got rid of the dog. He's gone.'

'Gone!' squealed the young rats, whisking their tails and darting to and fro. 'The dog's gone, the dog's gone!'

'Gone down the river,' said the Njimbin, nodding and grinning. 'So now you can move up into the dry.'

'Good news,' said the older rats, but they went on looking cautious and twitching their whiskers. The Njimbin hid its irritation.

'Good shelter under the people's house,' it pointed

out. 'Not patchy like this. You'll be snug and dry before the rain settles in, and handy to the old woman's garden. Never mind the thanks; don't I always look after my friends?'

'Ah,' said an old rat, 'the Njimbin's a good friend. And when the rain settles we'll come.'

'Glad of the shelter,' said another. 'Only now the guavas are coming on.'

'And the young bracken and the raspberries,' said a third. 'No bracken up at the cottage.'

The Njimbin laughed kindly. 'Young bracken, eh? And what about pumpkin seeds? What about tomatoes and locquats?'

The old rats laughed too, and knocked a couple of younger ones off a branch for the sake of discipline. 'He's a funny man, this Njimbin,' they told each other. 'Pumpkin seeds are *inside* the cottage.' 'Locquats are still green, hard as stones.' 'Tomato seeds haven't sprouted yet.' They chuckled and nodded.

The Njimbin frowned darkly. 'And don't I fetch and carry for you? Don't I see you have the best of everything?'

The old rats were quick to agree. 'Best of everything. We got a good friend in the Njimbin. Be moving back up the ridge any day now,' they promised soothingly. But the Njimbin was not soothed, for it knew the old rats were sly and cunning; that was how they had lived to become old rats.

On its way up the ridge it remembered how the old woman had mended the fowlhouse. That was a more cheering thought: to be warm and dry, with the door closed and no rain coming through the roof. And how

45

the old woman had worked to make a dry camp for the Njimbin! It chuckled and regained its swagger and felt superior to the rats. It had latched the fowlhouse door behind it and was half-way to its favourite perch before it noticed the warmth and life in the place, or saw the white shapes in the dark.

The hens were asleep with their heads buried under their wings on a lower rung of the perches. The rooster, as was only right, had taken his lordly place on the top, the Njimbin's own perch. The Njimbin snarled and sprang.

The rooster woke in the act of falling and gargled with shock, trumpeting with outrage. The hens woke and screamed for help. The rooster cackled to them to keep calm and stay out of his way; he arched his neck and drooped his wings in the dark, and began a war dance on the earth of the fowlhouse floor. The Njimbin, still off-balance from its leap, fell off its perch into the war-dance.

The hens shrieked, 'Oh help, oh help, quick, quick, quick!' The rooster tried to spur and trample the Njimbin. All the frogs within hearing began to bellow, 'What? What? What?' The Njimbin, having slid aside as quick as a spirit can, reached for its weapons: they were not there, having been hidden from Mrs Tucker. Forced to improvise, it planted a hard kick under the rooster's gracefully curved tail and leapt back to its perch.

'Treachery! Scandal! Who? Where?' trumpeted the rooster.

'Thick-head!' cried the Njimbin in wordless fury. 'Do you want your scrawny neck wrung?'

'Oh help, oh fox, oh fire!' sobbed the hens.

'What? What? What?' bellowed the frogs.

The rooster trampled about in the dark, threatening

and searching. Finding nothing, it tried to fly back to its perch. The Njimbin was ready for it and knocked it down again, and the whole performance was repeated except that this time the Njimbin kept its place on the perch.

In the end all the fowls spent the night huddled on the floor in the farthest corner of the fowlhouse. The Njimbin, crouching grimly above, kept them awake with threats and insults. Most of the threats were empty, for the fowls were too big for it to handle without weapons, but its rage made it terrible to them. In the first grey light they raced out to their yard and ran about restlessly in the rain, sobbing to each other. They were still inclined to be hysterical when Mrs Tucker brought their morning mash.

She was disappointed but not suspicious to find them in this state, for her mind was full of worry about Hector. She told herself that the fowls were strangers to each other as well as to their run, and were still fighting out their new pecking order. She did not see a grey shadow crouched behind the nest-box; she did not even notice last night's wheat uneaten in the yard. She simply squeezed handfuls of mash to make sure it was properly crumbly and tossed it to the fowls and went away. The fowls did not have even the calming influence of breakfast, for they were used to modern, labour-saving pellets. The man in the produce store had mentioned this to Mrs Tucker; she had merely replied, '*Tchut!*' and bought good, reliable feed. So now the mash lay among the wheat while the fowls paced restlessly in the rain.

Mrs Tucker put on the old raincoat, slipped a plastic bag over the white cone of her hair, took up the bent wattle stick, and set off to look for Hector. The sky was still deeply cushioned in cloud and showers wandered over the ridges. Kangaroos and wallabies, kept out late by the rainy light, went bouncing away in no particular hurry. Mrs Tucker's gumboots squelched in water that ran hidden under the grass. Small frogs imitated the sound of rain and patches of lobelia imitated pools. From an old habit, learnt when her children were young, Mrs Tucker went first to the river; and so she discovered that her boat too was missing.

She thought about this in a puzzled way while she searched and called. In the scrub, water dripped heavily from branches; the air was full of the sharp, strong smell of lantana, and clouds of mosquitoes rose from the wet litter. Mrs Tucker had to break off a twig of green leaves to beat the mosquitoes away from her nose and mouth. There was no sign of Hector.

The boat ... surely he'd never get into that? He wouldn't even go near the river, it was stupid to look. But if someone had taken him ... and taken the boat too ... it was funny that they were both missing. She remembered Hector backing away and howling when she herself tried to coax him into the boat: would he have given in if she had tried harder? Very likely; a person's own dog did give in at last – but not to a stranger. A stranger would have to catch him, tie him up and drag him aboard. It was such a far-fetched idea that she gave it up; the boat had simply come adrift and Hector was somewhere else. She went on searching and calling.

Meanwhile the Njimbin crouched on its perch and brooded darkly. In all its years of living among people they had never given it so much trouble; the old people had respected it, the new ones had never known it was there at all. Their dogs had been banished from the house at night – chained up, unprotected, easily cowed and trained. Making use of the people, taking steps to correct their more troublesome ways and adapting to the more harmless, the Njimbin had always been secretly in control. No one had ever invaded its camps for it chose them carefully; the fowlhouse had been empty and tumbling down for years before the Njimbin had quietly moved in. Only this old woman, with her pesty dog and her crotchety ideas about fowls, had upset the Njimbin's control. It was deeply affronted.

The fowls were in a bad temper; they squabbled and pecked at each other and ran about the yard shrieking, and the Njimbin glowered. But in quieter moments, as the twilit morning went on, it became aware of other tiny sounds. Its eyes and ears sharpened.

There were rustles in the blady-grass – a flicker near the fence – a sly nibbling at the base of a wall. The Njimbin climbed down quietly and stole out to the fowlyard.

'No, no, no, no, no!' cried the hens when they saw its gnarled little figure. The rooster shouted, 'What's this, what's this?' and herded the hens safely into a corner. The Njimbin, gathering up wheat and mash, only said gruffly, 'Well, *you* don't want it.'

The Njimbin had decided that it would have to co-exist with the fowls for a while. If wheat and mash could draw the rats up from the young bracken, there would have to be wheat and mash; in the Njimbin's own hands.

7 🌿

By afternoon there were no more showers wandering about the Broad. Sunlight came filtering through the clouds and lit wet trees and grass till they sparkled. Mrs Tucker wanted to go out again and look for Hector, but her bunions and her back ached from the long morning's search and she had to put her feet up and rest. She lay on her bed and grumbled about the noise from the fowlrun: 'What's got into the maggoty things?' Sometimes she got up and went to a window in case Hector had dragged himself home; then she would mutter, 'Snake-bite or I'm a Dutchman,' and go and lie down again.

She knew a grown woman should not fret over a missing dog; that instead she should pull on her gumboots and go out to soothe the fowls, removing whatever it was – a blowing feather, an inquisitive magpie – that was upsetting them. But she felt tired and worried and alone, and a cold little doubt had somehow crept into her mind. Maybe, after all, she was too old to live free and independent in the country and keep fowls. Maybe she was just a silly old woman, going soft in the head, who had run away from a good safe home like a naughty child.

She did go out at last to give the fowls their wheat, and was glad to see them pecking it up eagerly and driving each other out of the way. Since she did not know that they had already missed two meals, she thought this was a good sign and the maggoty things were settling down at last. On her tired old feet, and leaning on her bent stick, she went down into the gully among paperbark trees to have another look for Hector.

She had already looked in most of the places she could reach. She only wandered and called and listened for a howl or yelp. Now that the rain had gone the insects were out in force. The air was busy with flies and moths and butterflies; wherever she paused a new swarm of mosquitoes arose; tiny midges drifted in columns like smoke; hunting dragonflies flew in squadrons. A torn and twisted scrap of paperbark lay caught on a leaf; Mrs Tucker poked at it idly with a finger and found it was a moth – a whole and living moth, all its symmetry and shape cunningly hidden. It was suddenly frightening, this sly concealment of shape. It meant that anything could really be something else. Mrs Tucker hobbled quickly home.

That night a cloud of small insects whirled about the kitchen light, and lace-wings that came to prey on them hung fragile and long-legged on the kitchen wall. It seemed impossible to keep them out. Through the gauzed open window came a burst of hysterical cackling from the fowlrun; Mrs Tucker muttered *tchut* and *tchah*. She opened the back door and switched on the light over the step, to scare off any fox that might be prowling; a tide of little cream moths flowed upward to the light. She switched it off quickly and shut the door, but she knew that the tide of fluttering wings now washed and flowed outside all the screens.

She felt alone, cut off, and went to bed to hide in the dark. But when the light had gone, the tiny beetles and midges were drawn to white surfaces that loomed in the dark; they found her pillow and moved like thistledown over her face and crawled in her hair. Mrs Tucker retreated head and all under the sheet. She could hear, very close to her ear, the mosquito-hum of the midges – a sound so fine that it lay on the very edge of hearing.

Outside, the moths too had settled on the white walls of the cottage. The bat that lived in the shed gave up hunting them, and a fat spider whose web was filled could now deal with its catch. The rats came tunnelling through the blady-grass and prowled along the wire netting of the fowlyard. Two or three of them began to mine the walls. The Njimbin smiled and came out of the wild tobacco.

'Ho, old friends! Guavas finished, are they? Ah, well: a windy diet, guavas and bracken shoots; you want better, with the wet weather coming on. Try some of this. Best of everything up here.' It tilted a rusty jam-tin and poured little heaps of wheat and mash into the grass.

The young rats squealed and pounced, squabbling over the heaps and driving each other off. The old rats bowled the young ones over and shouldered them out of the way.

'Where are all these melons and tomatoes, then?' they teased the Njimbin, with their mouths full and their whiskers covered in mash. 'Don't see any garden. Fowls, isn't it? Lost your camp, old friend?'

The young rats, trying to sneak in between the tails of

52

their elders, sniggered. The Njimbin laughed falsely.

'Lost my camp – what do you take me for? Feather warmers for winter and an egg when I want it, that's what I've got. Good company, too. But don't you worry, I'm too good-natured to forget my friends. Now the dog's gone you can shift up here and get fat and sleek on fowlfeed.'

'Ah,' said the old rats wisely, crunching wheat. 'Rain's gone, it seems.'

'Working up to more, you mean.' The Njimbin made secret signs to the hungry young rats and slyly tipped a special heap of feed for them behind the dark corner of the fowlhouse. It drew back into the wild tobacco and reached for its waddy, waiting. The old rats, having cleaned up all the other heaps, rubbed their full bellies and went back to mining the fowlhouse walls. The stars shone clean and bright between ragged clouds.

Morning, when it came, was polished like a pearl. Swamp-oaks and cobwebs were silver with dew; mist lay deep on the Broad and trailed in wisps between the blue hills beyond. Grass and weeds that had baked in the heat were already green and lush. Under the mist a trawler thudded in from the river. Mrs Tucker, throwing mash to the fowls, thought it sounded very near; so near that when the thud of the engine stopped she wondered if some fisherman had found her missing boat. She threw the last of the mash to the fowls and began to walk down to the river, just in case.

In the mist sound travelled as clearly as sunlight in the rain-washed air. Someone was rowing, a strong rower: Mrs Tucker heard the oars in the rowlocks and even the clucking of water against the boat. Trawlers trawled, of course; did they also set nets? Mrs Tucker hobbled a little faster. She heard the oars shipped, the boat knocking against something, the rowing begin again and draw away. Some business of their own, she decided, as the trawler's engine started up; but there was no harm in looking, they wouldn't fine you for that.

The mist thickened near the river. She came through it to the bank where the dinghy had been tied – and there was *Agnes* bobbing in the mist at the length of its mooring line; and in it Hector sitting upright and withdrawn, home yet not home, expecting nothing.

'Well – I – *never*!' cried Mrs Tucker with her old-blue eyes alight. She seized the line that was tied to an overhanging branch and pulled the boat in. 'Hector!' she boomed joyfully. 'Come out of that!'

Hector came in a bound. He stood drooping his white-plumed tail and his black ears, expecting to be punished. When Mrs Tucker battered him affectionately about the head and shoulders, he looked up at her with melting brown eyes and sat down hard on her feet.

'Get up, you old goat!' she cried, delighted. Hector sighed deeply and stayed where he was, so she gave him a push. At that he stood up and leaned heavily against her legs, causing her to stagger and catch at the branch. She responded to these signs of affection by beating his head again with one hand while, with the other, she pushed the boat out on the falling tide. It was a dangerous operation that nearly ended with both of them in the water. When it was over Mrs Tucker pulled herself upright again, nearer to six feet tall than she had been while Hector was missing, and looked at him fondly.

'And what in creation happened to you?' she demanded.

54

Hector made no attempt to explain as some dogs might have done, either with body-movements or with barks. He only beat his tail once or twice in the wild geranium. He was always a better listener than talker and preferred simply to listen to Mrs Tucker. For a moment Mrs Tucker had nothing to say; she was puzzled and even a little troubled. It was clear that Hector had, after all, gone voyaging in the boat, and how this could have happened she could not in any way imagine.

'Well,' she said at last, 'enough's enough. We'll go home. You'll be needing breakfast.'

They went home. Hector stayed close at heel all the way. He did not in fact need breakfast, for cane-growers and fishermen had fed him; but he accepted breakfast as a reward for coming home and ate it readily. Afterwards Mrs Tucker took him out to meet the fowls.

They were scratching busily in their yard, but as soon as they saw Mrs Tucker they crowded against the wire netting, trampling each other and shouting each other down. 'Oh help, oh food, oh hungry!' they cried. 'Me, me, me quick, quick!' And when she threw them the handful of shellgrit she had brought they fell on it with real hunger.

Hector was startled and affronted to find these large birds making noisy demands on his revered person. He turned this way and that along the netting, offering to put the birds into the air and rid Mrs Tucker of them; but she would not allow it and gave him a light cuff on the nose.

'No,' she boomed sternly. 'You let them alone. Dogs can't lay eggs, remember.' But she was puzzled and troubled again, for she had just fed the fowls with a generous meal of mash and every scrap had vanished.

How could they be hungry? She stayed frowning over the problem while Hector wandered off in a huff, and was only roused by an unexpected sound from the shed: Hector was growling, deep and dangerous.

She hobbled quickly after him, calling. He was standing before a large tool-chest in a corner of the shed, his powerful body gathered on its short legs ready to spring and a crest of hair standing rigid on his spine. He had something cornered behind the box, and as Mrs Tucker arrived the growl changed to a rattling snarl. She thought instantly of snakes.

'Hector, come out of that!' she shouted. 'You'll be bitten.'

Hector only leaned into his shoulders and snarled again. Something – not a snake, more like a giant rat – scuttled into the shadows under the work-bench, and Hector hurtled out of the shed almost knocking Mrs Tucker over as he went. She hurried out. He was making angry rushes at the trunk of a bloodwood tree, growling threats and barking defiance in turn.

'I'll gr-r-rind you to gr-r-ristle,' Hector threatened.

'Why don't you go and swim in the river?' jeered the Njimbin from high in the tree.

'No-stink! Lemme at you! Come down and fight!'

The little rats hid in the blady-grass and were full of wicked joy: their dear old friend the Njimbin had tripped on his own whiskers this time.

'Hector!' bellowed Mrs Tucker, peering into the tree for a goanna or a bird. 'Will you come out of that!'

'Oh help, oh fire, oh fox!' yelled the hens, flapping to and fro in the fowlyard. 'Volcano! Hawk, hawk, hawk!'

It took Mrs Tucker some time to bully Hector away from the bloodwood tree and back into the cottage. She had never seen him angry before and didn't know what to make of it. She had to make another cup of tea and sit down to drink it, looking at him sternly.

'What got into you, then?' she demanded.

He gave her a dark, sad look that might have been suffering or reproachful or deeply shamed, but Mrs Tucker didn't see it. She was remembering the hungry fowls and wondering whether she should feed them again. There were too many funny things going on, too many puzzles for a slow old mind.

In the afternoon the clouds built up again. Mrs Tucker and Hector went prowling as usual, and Hector snuffled busily through stands of bracken, tangles of raspberry and springing tufts of wire-grass. It was good to have him back, and Mrs Tucker sat on a log to watch and smile; but the smile faded and she grew a little depressed. Something had changed.

It seemed that Hector no longer went racing joyfully through the tangles after lizards or came bounding up to check on his direction; he no longer hurled himself into the air after birds or butterflies. Now he hunted intently, pushing his way into flood debris and among fallen branches and into thickets of young wattle. Once he rushed at a burnt-out hollow log and snarled and barked with that new anger he had shown in the morning. Whatever funny thing had taken him off on that mysterious voyage, Mrs Tucker decided that it had done him no good.

Hector was an embittered dog.

8 ❧

The Njimbin too was embittered.

It had used all its wits and energy to care for its ungrateful stock. It had trapped the rat-hunting dog into the boat and taken it away to the loneliest of islands – and now the dog had returned and hunted the Njimbin. It had endured the invasion of noisy, feather-headed fowls and industriously gathered up their feed to delight the rats. And what had it got in return? The rats chose to stay in their waterlogged gully though they knew the wet weather was near, and they accepted the Njimbin's gifts with sly taunts and jeers.

'Narrow squeak today, eh?' they had said, with their mouths full of stolen mash. 'Thought he had you that time.'

'We take it very kindly,' they had said, gnawing wheat, 'you drawing him off like that for our good.' And the young ones had tittered and whisked their tails.

'Don't know why you didn't drown him when you had the chance,' the elders had said kindly. 'Saved you a lot of trouble, that would.'

'Have you ever tried to drown a dog?' the Njimbin had

58

been driven to retort. 'Dogs can swim, even if they are scared of water.'

'Ah,' the elders had said thoughtfully. 'What about fowls, then? Will they drown?'

And, grinning behind their whiskers, they had gone back to work tunnelling into the fowlhouse so that they could gather their own mash and wheat without the Njimbin's help. They had already achieved two neat entries, but the Njimbin had stuffed one of them full of stones and pushed the hens' nesting-box on top of the other.

So when, in the night, the Njimbin heard the beat of rain on the iron just over its head, it only listened sourly and pushed the rooster off his perch again. It would not go down to the gully and offer to help the rats move out before they drowned; it would not be teased by elders and sniggered at by juniors. Let them drown; there were always lizards and frogs.

Left to themselves, the little black rats came swarming up from the gully of their own accord, for they knew that this time the rain was in earnest and they did need shelter.

'Don't worry about the dog,' they told each other with twinkling eyes. 'He's too busy chasing the Njimbin.'

'Ah,' they agreed with each other, 'a Clever Man, our good old friend Njimbin is. And we don't want to miss all those melons and tomatoes in that garden.'

In twos and threes they skittered uphill through their blady-grass tunnels. They re-explored the shed, finding dark dry corners behind tools and on rafters; pickings of grass seed on rakes; a bundle of old rags for nest-linings; a bottle of linseed oil that leaked a little when it was tipped

59

over. They burrowed in the dry ground under the cottage, squabbling over the most sheltered spots. They rediscovered dusty playgrounds within the cottage walls: old routes along scantling, old toys of bones and banksia-cones left behind in summer, old enemies to tease and be chased by in the big, hairy huntsman spiders. The rats were so pleased and excited, they raced and climbed and squabbled and bumped so noisily, that they woke Mrs Tucker.

She was dreaming: she was down at the river with young Ivan, who was trying to untie the boat. 'It won't come,' he said. 'I tied it with a screw-thatchet.'

'This way,' said Mrs Tucker, and gave the mooring line a jerk. It came free. 'Now in you hop,' she said to Hector. He rolled on his back and pleaded with his front paws, but she was firm. 'Get a move on,' she said, ordering him into the boat. 'I have to give the fowls their second breakfast.'

'You can't,' said young Ivan. 'You haven't given them the first yet. See?' He arranged some stones in a pattern on the ground to prove it.

'That's a funny thing,' said Mrs Tucker suspiciously, but young Ivan laughed and laughed, throwing his stones into the boat.

'Don't you know you're going off your head?' he shouted.

Mrs Tucker woke with a jerk. It took her a heart-stopping moment to realize that the lively bumping and scampering in her walls was not being made by young Ivan. Then she muttered, 'Rats! Maggoty things,' and hammered on the wall. The rats fell silent for a moment, considering this. Then they began again.

It was very irritating. Mrs Tucker lay awake for some time listening to the noise. She banged again once or twice with the same result as before, and tossed and turned till at last the noise stopped of its own accord. She told herself as she dozed off again that it was probably rats that upset the fowls and Hector. She wondered sleepily if John Bright had kept any traps. It did not occur to her to wonder why the noisy games in the wall had suddenly stopped, or to guess that the rats had discovered the fowls' wheat.

The bags of dry mash, shellgrit and wheat still stood in the back porch near Hector's basket. The old floor, weathered long ago when the porch was still an open verandah, had one or two boards a little rotted and broken. The rats who were nest-building under the cottage had found these boards, and caught the smells of wheat and of Hector that came through. They went to work very cautiously, reminding each other not to wake the dog.

They gnawed away at the edge of a board till a snout could reach the tough brown paper above. One tooth-hole in the paper was enough: a fine trickle of wheat grains began to slither through. The news spread quickly.

Hector and Mrs Tucker slept on. The Njimbin grumbled at the fowls. The clouds threw down another shower.

9 🌿

It was still raining when Mrs Tucker woke. The rats were all sleeping in dry nests with their stomachs full of wheat. The only sounds were the hush of rain on the roof, the thump-thump of Hector scratching, and an outburst of squabbling from the fowls in their run. A line of scurrying ants was climbing the kitchen wall, appearing through a join in the skirting and vanishing into the door-frame, endlessly moving like people on an escalator. It was not a cheerful morning, and Mrs Tucker found herself remembering her neat, bright room at Sunset House. There the weather was something to look at and talk about; it was not allowed to interfere with life.

She was shocked to find herself thinking such a thing and at once grew cheerful and talkative. 'Out you go and pedal your bike,' she ordered Hector as she flung open the back door. 'You're not a sugar dog, you won't melt.'

Hector humped his long body down the step quite willingly; he didn't mind water in the form of rain. Mrs Tucker mixed a bowl of mash, put on her rain gear and pulled the plastic bag over her topknot, and went out to feed the fowls.

They were scratching about dejectedly with the rain

dripping off their feathers. Their yellow eyes had a glassy look and the rooster's head was drooping. They hurtled into action when they saw Mrs Tucker, and trampled each other against the wire calling for food. Mrs Tucker gave it to them and stayed to watch them eat it, shaking her head at them in a worried way.

'You look like a yard of pumpwater,' she told them. 'Maggoty rats stealing your food or I'm a Dutchman.'

Crouching behind the nest-box, the Njimbin glowered. But the fowls gobbled and fought, making whistling noises as they choked themselves with mash; it was bound to make the old woman suspicious. And the Njimbin could not get to work while she stood there watching. The rats would have to make do with potato peelings and pumpkin seeds for a while.

Mrs Tucker filled the water-trough and took Hector off for his walk; but the plastic bag dripped water down the back of her neck, and Hector stopped often to shake himself free of water, and soon they went home. Mrs Tucker began a letter to her daughter Helen.

All day grey curtains of rain swept across the ridges and the Broad. Sometimes the sun struck down between them, lighting up raindrops threaded on oak-needles. All green things began to grow; branches reached out and filled with leaves, creepers and vines clambered over grasses, buds began to fill. Mrs Tucker and Hector sheltered in the cottage. The Njimbin, unhampered, went to and fro gathering a store of good things and stole under the cottage to count rat-holes.

In the evening Mrs Tucker threw wheat to the fowls and stayed to watch them eat it. She held no discussions with them and her eyes were clouded and old; for her mind, pushing ideas about, had offered her two pictures to choose between. One, that seemed very unlikely, was of hordes of rats descending on the fowlrun at feeding time, cleaning up the feed from under the fowls' beaks before they had a chance to eat it. The second was more frightening: a picture of an old woman going senile, forgetting to do the things she thought she had done and doing others, crazy things, that she forgot she had done. She watched the fowls and brooded over these pictures while Hector trampled back and forth under the bloodwood tree, until at last she called him off and they went inside.

The Njimbin came down from the bloodwood tree and gathered together its store of berries and roots and seeds and young leaves for the rats. It had been to a good deal of trouble to collect their favourite foods, and in the grey evening, with rain rustling into the grass, the Njimbin slipped into the dry dark under the cottage and called to them.

'No fowlfeed tonight,' it told the rats cheerfully. 'Fowls are starving, eaten it all. Never mind, no need to get wet, I've been working for you all day. What about this lot?' And it spread the good things before them.

The rats were polite but not interested.

'Thanks, old friend, but we're all right. Don't you worry.' They nodded to each other and smoothed their whiskers. 'We got resources. No need to trouble you.' They picked among the roots and leaves. 'Windy stuff, this. Don't bother with it.'

The Njimbin was silent, staring at them from under its brows. It had known the tastes and preferences of their kind for centuries before any of them were born. Into the silence, from far back under the cottage, came a tiny slithering sound. The rats stole glances at each other and looked carelessly away.

The Njimbin slid into the deepest dark where the cottage came close to the ground. Two young rats who had been feasting there came scuttling back looking scared. The Njimbin was heard to give a silent cry: 'Thankless big-bellies!' Then it was gone.

The rats ran about for joy, frisking and jumping over each other and whisking their tails. They knew the Njimbin would be back – that drought would come again and that they would need its help – that even now, from behind any house-stump, a waddy might thud silently on to the skull of a careless rat; but this was the good time. They made the most of it.

There is no worse insult to a Njimbin than to make it look foolish, for it prides itself on its slyness and cunning. This Njimbin had been made to look foolish more than once; it was very angry. It rushed back to its camp, seizing its hidden spear as it went.

In the fowlhouse too it was almost dark. The fowls, well fed for the second time that day, were sleeping quietly: four dim white shapes on the perches. The Njimbin shoved the fowlhouse door wide open and leapt for them.

'Out!' it grunted as it tumbled them off the perches. 'Find your own camp.'

'What, what, what?' shouted the rooster, flapping in angry circles on the floor. All the hens shrieked and struggled to get back to their perches. Only the rain on the iron roof of the cottage could have hidden the noise from Mrs Tucker's ears.

The Njimbin gritted its teeth and made short sharp jabs with its spear. 'Get out! Eggless – earless – feather-legs. Get out.' It prodded and harried them towards the open door. One hen scuttled out shrieking, the other two followed sobbing, and the rooster sprang after them yelling, 'Run, run, run! Come back, come back!' and other instructions. The Njimbin latched the fowlhouse door and stood on guard outside.

It felt much better for having asserted itself. It listened to the fowls lamenting among bracken and blady-grass, losing themselves in thickets of wattle, finding each other and circling back towards home; and it frowned in a superior way.

'No-ears. Don't they know I've done them a favour?' It crept towards them through the dusk. 'Have to show 'em, that's all; can't help my good nature.'

It met the rooster stepping high through the tangles, leading his charges home. 'You're free, thick-head,' the Njimbin pointed out, and pricked him under the tail with the spear. The rooster whirled and went charging off into the dark. The hens scattered. The Njimbin slipped like a shadow after the nearest.

'Grubs and worms and beetles,' it promised, sending her off up the ridge.

'Find yourself a nice low branch,' it advised another, nudging her out of the long grass. Whichever way the fowls turned they found the Njimbin there. At last they drew on an ancient wisdom that they had not known they possessed: they stopped rushing about, wing-beating and calling to each other, and instead crouched low and still within thickets. When even the Njimbin's spirit-ears could hear nothing it went home in great satisfaction and shut itself into its camp.

The fowlhouse felt homely. The rain boomed on the roof; a meal of witchetty-grubs, which the Njimbin had discovered while it foraged for the rats, was hidden under the nest-box. The Njimbin roasted them on a small fire that it built in the farthest corner. When it had eaten them it climbed to its favourite perch and slept contentedly.

During the night the fowls crept back one by one, found each other, and huddled together outside the fowlhouse door. The Njimbin woke to hear them squabbling softly and comforting each other. Now that its temper had cooled it did not drive them off again, for it saw that they would always come back. But it refused to open the door, and spent the rest of the night jeering about creatures so poor-spirited that they returned to a prison where they had been starved and ill-treated. The fowls went on begging to be let in until Mrs Tucker arrived with their morning mash.

Mrs Tucker stared, frowning. She tested the door several times to make sure it was properly latched. She let the fowls in, fed them, closed the door and tested it several more times. She made no remark to the fowls or to Hector; she did not even say *tchut*, for she was not vexed. She was frightened.

That afternoon young Ivan came trudging up the ridge with her groceries, for he had not been allowed to ride his brother's motorcycle on the wet track. Mrs Tucker was still so frightened that she did not go at once to fetch his two dollars, she kept him waiting while she asked some questions, bribing him with biscuits. She made the questions sound as innocent as she could.

'Did you see my chooks?' Ivan, munching chocolate

creams, shook his head. 'Have a look as you go. Nice-looking birds but a flighty lot – not one egg yet. Something's upsetting them; rats, I shouldn't wonder, but it might be a goanna or a snake?'

Ivan marched off to the fowlrun. When she followed she found him searching along the base of the wire netting and walls. He lifted the nest-box: a neat burrow and two dead witchetty-grubs were revealed. Ivan looked triumphant.

'Well I never!' cried Mrs Tucker. 'A rat-hole sure enough! But how do the maggoty things get out with the box on top?'

Ivan examined the underside of the box. It was sound and whole. He hunched his shoulders, ground the heel of his boot into the rat-hole and put the box back in place. She'd asked about rats and there was the hole; what more did she want?

Mrs Tucker said quickly, 'I'll have to set some traps. I never heard fowls make such a fuss about a few rats – I was going to ask if you'd seen any strangers about. The track goes right near your house, doesn't it? You'd see any funny-looking stranger, someone who might be after a chook or an egg. There was the boat too – you heard it got away?'

Ivan looked hunted. Not only had he heard: he'd been soundly ribbed by his fisherman family for tying up a boat with a reef-knot and no one believed his angry denials.

'It never got loose with Hector in it,' said Mrs Tucker roundly. 'When it comes to boats, Hector's got a yellow streak a yard wide. But if some stranger was messing about with it, Hector might go in after him. You haven't seen anyone?'

Young Ivan brooded, but in the end he had to shake his head. Mrs Tucker produced his money and let him go. It hadn't been much use, she thought, with the chill of fear still inside her; she hadn't been able to bring herself to tell the child about Hector's angry hunting of some enemy she couldn't see, or about the fowlhouse door firmly latched with the fowls on the outside.

She kept her word about the traps. Ransacking the shed she found half a dozen, set them with baits of cheese, and placed them outside the walls of the fowlhouse. That night she listened for any outcry from the fowls; but all she could hear was rain, a sly rustling inside her walls, and then the scampering and bumping and gnawing of happy rats.

Mrs Tucker muttered *tchah* and hammered on the wall with a shoe. There was instant silence. Then, as though the rats had recognized that this was only silly old Mrs Tucker who didn't count, the noise began again. Mrs Tucker pressed her lips together. She had begun to feel that it was the rats who belonged here and she who was the intruder. She even wondered if they knew about the traps and were laughing at her.

There was no sound that she could hear from the fowlhouse. In sudden panic she told herself that it was too quiet: that maybe, for the second time, the fowls were shut out instead of in. She *knew* they were shut in when she had fed them – but she had known that last night too, and when you got old you got silly. A silly old woman living alone with a dog and going off her head . . . .

69

With shaking hands Mrs Tucker dragged on her raincoat and took up her stick. She went outside, not switching on a light but prodding her way across the yard with her stick and groping along the side of the shed, so that her eyes could pick out the shapes of fowls in the dark. She did not reach the fowlhouse; from the corner of the shed she could see it, and she stood quite still in the rain.

Through the crack of the door and the ill-fitting gap above it, spilling out into the fowlyard, she could see the flickering red-and-gold light of fire: a small, flickering fire making the fowlhouse cosy and domestic in the rain.

Mrs Tucker fled, hobbling back across the yard to the cottage. She lay shaking in bed until she was too tired to stay awake, and then she dreamed. She did not think of the fowls – she did not for a moment think that the fowlhouse itself was burning.

10

Mrs Tucker slept heavily at last and woke late, as people often do after a bad night. It took a moment to remember why she felt so out of sorts; then the cobweb of fear, the small puzzles and little dark doubts began to wind round her again. She pressed her old lips tightly together and got up frowning. If she was going off her head she had better do it neatly and carefully.

She put on one of John Bright's clean shirts and a fresh pair of overalls. She replaited her long white hair, twisted it into its cone-shaped topknot, and combed out the wisps that curled around her face. She sent Hector out to pedal his bike while she mixed the mash for the fowls. Then, straightening her bony shoulders, she went out to the fowlrun.

The clouds had climbed higher in the night and were tumbling across the sky. Down on the Broad a late shower swept after them. With her lips still tightly pressed together Mrs Tucker fed the fowls. Then, while they pecked and gobbled in the yard, she began a determined examination of the fowlhouse.

It looked just as usual. There was no sign of a fire or even of a shadow behind the nest-box, for the Njimbin

71

had slipped out of the open door. Mrs Tucker poked into the corners with her stick, and in one corner the tip of the stick lodged in a twist of wire. Mrs Tucker drew it out – a strong wire spring, blackened and dull, that looked familiar. Prodding and scraping in loosened earth she turned up bits of charred wood carefully buried, more blackened springs and some shapes of wire.

She dragged them outside into the light and carefully shut the door. She was almost more frightened than before, but she searched around the fowlhouse for the traps she had set. They had all disappeared.

Mrs Tucker stood frowning sternly. Then she gathered up the bits of wire and carried them back to the cottage.

She set them out in a row on the kitchen table. 'And *that's* no dream,' she said grimly to Hector. 'That's burnt rat-traps.'

Hector looked up at them with earnest brown eyes and beat his plumed tail on the floor. Not for a moment did he entertain the thought that a person who could shut fowls out and forget about it might also absent-mindedly light a fire and burn rat-traps. Mrs Tucker did entertain the thought, but it called for a complicated timetable: 1. set traps; 2. some time later collect traps and set alight; 3. go inside; 4. come out again while fire is still burning and discover it; 5. run away and go to bed; 6. come out again some time later and bury dead fire. It might be possible, but Mrs Tucker could only feel that it was unlikely.

'Still and all,' she told Hector, 'there's something funny going on.' And at once she felt stronger and better, for that much at least was proved: something strange and *real* was going on. She had not imagined that fire in the fowlhouse for here was the evidence on the kitchen table;

and it was solid and real, something you could handle and look at and show to someone else. Mrs Tucker felt so much better that she even thought about breakfast and began to set it out.

That was when she discovered the ants.

She was used to finding a few ants in the cottage, and especially since the rain began. They never seemed interested in her groceries; they only gathered the frail little corpses that fell from the kitchen light, or travelled their own invisible roads through her house. Mrs Tucker ignored them or swept them out. This morning she found a busy ant-road leading into her packet of breakfast food.

She made one of her disgusted spitting noises and dumped the packet into the kitchen sink. Ants came swarming out, and she saw that they came from between the cardboard packet and its greased-paper lining. They were not attacking the crisp flakes inside; they were, in fact, starting a new nest between the packet and its lining. Mrs Tucker had never known ants to behave in such a way. She exclaimed and tutted and cooked herself an egg.

Later, when she was sweeping the front verandah, she found a heap of soil, as much as a cupful, spilt from a pot in which she had planted wild violets. The plants were wilted, undermined by an army of tiny ants that had built themselves a nest inside the pot. Mrs Tucker's moustache bristled. She destroyed the nest by refilling the pot with earth and standing it in the laundry tub until the ants should give in and retreat.

She made her worst discovery when she came to make her bed. The bed stood near a wall and her blanket, thrown back to air, had slid into folds against it. As she lifted it a crowd of large black ants scurried out from the folds; it seemed that they too were in search of a nest and had chosen Mrs Tucker's blanket. It had been a determined choice: they had explored, discovered, investigated, and begun work in large numbers, all since Mrs Tucker had got up this morning.

She was thoroughly irritated. A raid on her sugar or jam would have been natural and right; but this business of selecting and taking over areas of her home was too much.

'We might as well not be here,' she complained to Hector. 'Catch them letting us make ourselves comfortable in *their* homes.' She seized a spray-can and sprayed all the ants she could find. Then, to escape from the spray, she took Hector out for a walk.

Down on the flat there were glints of water where the Broad, fed by rain and tide, had overflowed. In the gullies and on the ridges the grass stood tall, tangled with little flowering vines. Mrs Tucker had to wade through it slowly, prodding with her stick. Hector had to burrow through it with only his tail showing like a periscope. Under the grass, in a secret green world of guinea-flower, raspberry and wild geranium, he found again the busy roads of mice, hares, bandicoots and spiders; he rustled and whuffled after them, intent and eager if not with the old wild joy. Mrs Tucker smiled a little: perhaps the bad time was over. Perhaps all the funny things would be explained or forgotten; maybe Hector had only been upset at losing her, and she had been only frightened silly, and they were both recovering. She waded slowly up the ridge on her bunions while Hector's tail drew near, and turned away, and headed back again.

Then, from under a spread of lantana, she heard his angry growl and the fierce rattling snarl. Her heart leapt – it was all happening again, and she caught Hector's anger and bellowed to him: 'Send it, boy!'

At her word Hector sprang, snarling and yapping. He had something at bay – or he was at bay; she hobbled nearer, seeing only the lantana and all the tangled green, and Hector leaping through it and over it, backing off and leaping forward again. He sprang towards a stringybark tree, leapt up at it furiously, and barked and hurled himself at it again.

'He's treed it,' muttered Mrs Tucker, pushing herself ahead with her stick. She stood under the tree and peered up into branches against grey sky.

She could see nothing. She moved round the tree while Hector barked and bounced underneath. There was a movement up there, obscured by the drooping leaves; she remembered that goannas keep moving round the trunk, circling it to use it as a screen. She did not believe Hector would be angry over a goanna, but she moved forward again, turned quickly, and hobbled back. She thought she saw another flash of movement but she could not pick out a shape.

Something fell out of the tree, fast and hard like a stone, and thudded deep into the grass. Mrs Tucker moved as quickly as she could, but Hector was already snuffling at the spot. She reached it and got down awkwardly on her knees to fumble in the grass. Then she crouched there, staring.

What had fallen from the tree into the grass was a stone axe – a very small stone axe.

Mrs Tucker had never seen such a thing before, but

there was no mistaking it: the stone head chipped to shape and ground to an edge on both sides; the tough vine handle looped over the haft and hardened with age, bound tight with cord and cemented with gum. It was certainly a stone axe. And it had come tumbling out of the tree into which Hector had chased his secret enemy. And it had landed with a thud that shook all Mrs Tucker's thoughts into a jumble of jigsaw pieces.

After a moment she picked it up uncertainly. Then she got stiffly to her feet and began to hobble home. She did not ask herself a lot of useless questions or even try to think; her mind seemed to be quite blank. But after a time it began to look at the jigsaw pieces of thought; slowly, one by one.

And the first thing she thought was that the axe was real. It was here, in her hands. Like the burnt bits of rat-trap she could feel it and hold it and show it to someone else.

And the second thing she thought was that since it was real, it had really come out of the tree. And there was one thing a silly old woman who was going off her head could not possibly do: she could not climb a stringybark tree, drop a stone axe, and rush down the tree again to pick it up.

After that she thought how small the axe was. A man could never have used it. Yet it was a proper axe, efficient and made with slow care – surely not a toy for a small child?

By this time Mrs Tucker had reached home. She did not even look at the teapot but put the axe quickly on the kitchen table and went to lie down. She felt that her mind was about to make some sort of picture out of the jigsaw, and she wanted to leave it alone and not to peep.

In an hour or so she got up to have a little lunch. By then the jigsaw had made not quite a picture but at any rate a shape. She did not want to see it any more clearly, but while she made herself an apple sandwich she thought about the shape.

Something that made Hector angry, but only since his voyage in the boat. Something he had met under fallen branches, in a hollow log, behind tools in the shed; something Hector had seen when she had seen only a shadow or a movement.

Something small and fast, and tricky enough to trap Hector in the boat.

It owned a small stone axe, a thing from the past. It harried the fowls, turned them out of their run, made a fire in the fowlhouse and burnt the traps that had been placed around it.

Something small and fast and tricky and ancient, that lived in the fowlhouse.

That was all Mrs Tucker tried to know. Yet she felt that in some unseen way she knew this thing very well: a secret, ancient thing, small yet somehow immense and unknowable. It had to do, she thought, with the impertinence of rats and the disregard of ants; with fragile lime-green butterflies that ate up a whole tree; with the implacability of night, that rejected her but lay in wait for her cottage lights; with the sudden strong voices of frogs living hidden in pipes and gutters that she thought were only hers; even with the inscrutability of a twisted bit of paperbark that was really a living moth. All these things were in some way a part of this one small thing, and this thing challenged her.

Mrs Tucker stood up, almost six feet tall, and set the stone axe in plain sight on the shelf above the stove.

'We'll see about that,' she told Hector, with a glint in her old-blue eyes.

11

As soon as Mrs Tucker had gone off with the axe and
Hector had followed grumbling, the Njimbin slid down
from the stringybark tree and danced in pure rage. A
stone axe is a valuable tool; it takes skill and hard work
and the luck of the right stone to make. The Njimbin had
cherished this one for two hundred years and knew its
weight and balance as well as it knew the thrust of its own
knees.

'Thief!' it howled, making little spearing rushes after
the old woman. 'Fowl-lover! No-ears! Rat-trapper!' It
stamped its feet in the wild geranium and howled again in
pain, for last night one of Mrs Tucker's traps had caught it
by the toe.

The Njimbin had already treated the toe by thrusting it
into an ants' nest; and while the ants swarmed over it
biting and stinging, the Njimbin had spoken in silence to
the profound single mind of the nest. It had spoken of a
long time of rain, of soggy tunnels and drowned eggs, and
of warm, dry shelter in the old woman's cottage. Later,
when it had burnt the traps and rubbed ashes on the toe
to help the cure, it had spoken the same message to the
ant-minds of other nests. This small revenge had been

enough, for when rats and old women meet there are bound to be traps. Now something more was needed; the Njimbin sat nursing its toe and brooding.

It had never been a spirit of great power. There were some, as small in size, that might have attacked the old woman with illness or accident; some that might have brought against her the power of the land itself. These might have faced her openly and taken back the axe. That was not the Njimbin's way: it was slyer, more secretive, a being of smaller power. But it knew how to build terror out of small things. It knew that ordinary, expected things, if they behaved in an unexpected way, could start a little unreasonable fear that went jumping along the nerves; and unreason was the dark that turned fear into terror. The Njimbin could be terrible when its rage lasted long enough and the moment was right.

By and by it got to its feet and went swiftly, limping only a little, under the long grass to the old wombat burrow where its weapons and tools were hidden. It drew forth a woven-grass dillybag, tipped out a broken knife-blade, a yam and several pieces of stone, and went off with the bag towards the gully. On its way past the cottage it paused long enough to jam stones and broken bricks under the hole where the wheat trickled through, blocking the flow.

The big green frogs had been silent since the first showers of rain, for after the choruses were sung they had all gone in search of each other. But the Njimbin knew where to look in the gullies and swamps and dams, where silvery froths of eggs were moored to grass-stems and reeds. It did not waste time in persuading the frogs, for it knew they were a self-centred race and their minds were their own. The boggy pools and the trickles of water under grass would be gone soon enough; the frogs would not leave till they were ready to be lonely again. The Njimbin simply caught them and stuffed them into its dillybag.

The Njimbin knew a loose screen, that could be forced aside a little, on one of the cottage windows; and a broken board under the laundry tubs where the waste-pipe went through.

Mrs Tucker spent most of the day in the shed, searching for an old padlock and key that she thought she had seen somewhere there. She found it at last, in a rusty tin among the jars of nails and screws, and tested and oiled it. Then she had to remove the screws from a sliding bolt on one of the cupboard doors and screw it instead to the fowlhouse door; for, as she explained to Hector, her dander was up. When she had made all these arrangements she took Hector into the fowlhouse, where he nosed about a little looking puzzled, while the hens clucked and tutted in protest. From this Mrs Tucker deduced that the small tricky thing, whatever it might be, was not at home or Hector would have been angry. She called him out again, shot the bolt on the door and padlocked it, and put the key in her overalls pocket. Then, with the glint of triumph in her eyes, she went inside to rest.

As she pushed open the screen door she was startled by a hoarse yell of pain: *arrch!*

'Oh my goodness!' cried Mrs Tucker, letting the door bang closed. Hector, at once alert, forced himself between the door and her legs and almost knocked her over. After a moment she ventured to push again cautiously at the door. Hector shoved his nose into the gap and pushed harder. Mrs Tucker put her own head through; by now she had recognized the sound and knew what to expect.

The big green frog had been caught by the opening door as it hopped across the porch. Hector was now inside and nosing at it; it took a short leap away from his nose. This proved that it could still function, and indeed the gap under the door could not have pinched more than a leg, but Mrs Tucker did not like to hear any creature yell in pain.

'Poor thing,' she said uneasily, and pushed it outside as gently as she could with the hair-broom. She did not wonder why, in a lush wet world ideal for frogs, this one should have come into her dry cottage.

She did wonder this when she found three more frogs in the bathroom: one in the bath, one in a corner behind the door, and one under the handbasin. All had moulded themselves firmly into their corners as frogs do; all their yellow eyes were veiled and their leather throats pumping. Mrs Tucker caught them easily one by one and put them outside. Then she took a firm grip of her own chin and stood sharp-eyed and frowning.

Ants have their eggs to keep dry; they often invade houses in wet weather, and they generally travel in crowds. Frogs are different.

By the time Mrs Tucker had disturbed a frog clinging to her bedroom curtains and lost it in one of the front rooms, had removed another from among the bottles in the bottom of the kitchen cupboard, and had startled another in the damp dark under the sink, her moustache had begun to bristle. She glanced at the shelf above the stove: the axe was still there, and the bits of burnt rat-trap that she had put with it.

She had never thought of frogs as startling or alarming creatures, but she found it unsettling to have them leaping suddenly from unexpected places. She also found that one frog at a time may be easy to deal with but three or four are impossible. When Hector's feeding time arrived she was cautious, for his bag of dog-food was kept in the dank, dark cupboard under the laundry tubs. Mrs Tucker opened the door slowly and used her torch.

There were no fewer than six frogs moulding themselves into corners and the curves of the waste-pipe. They too were uneasy and suspicious; they had just been shoved into this strange place through a rough-edged hole that was too small for comfort, and they wanted only the silken tug of water and the slither of a worm down the throat. It was not possible to remove the dog-food without upsetting them.

Younger and more agile people than Mrs Tucker would have acted as she did: making clumsy rushes from side to side, throwing the flashlight, beating with the broom, bellowing, 'Maggoty vermin!' and, 'Send 'em boy!'; tripping over Hector and bellowing again; knocking over a kitchen chair and banging doors as the chase moved through the house. Hector helped: bouncing like a ball from frog to frog and losing them all; shoving between Mrs Tucker's legs and standing on her bunions; yelping with excitement as the chase went on; scratching and burrowing into corners all over the house long after the frogs were lost.

From under the cottage the Njimbin listened, hugging

itself with delight. The rats were not there to admire and applaud, but even that was satisfying. Since the Njimbin had cut off their supply of wheat the rats were out foraging for berries and roots – and another late shower was making it certain that they would all have wet fur. The Njimbin was thoroughly pleased with itself as it slipped through the dark and the rain to its own dry camp. Swarming up the fowlhouse door to reach the latch, it even thought kindly of the feathery warmth of the fowls.

It was a long time since it had seen either a bolt or a padlock. It did not remember them at first and was puzzled as it tried to open the door. When it did remember, of course it flew into a rage. It scrambled down and found a large stone, climbed up again and began to batter the padlock.

The fowls woke up and chattered to each other in sleepy alarm: 'What, what, what?' 'Oh no, oh who? Oh help, help, help!' But the padlock did not snap open, for the Njimbin had to cling on with one hand while it groped and battered in the dark with the other. Even so it might have managed – but as it paused to change its grip the blady-grass rustled and an old rat called politely.

'Locked out, old friend? That's a shame, that is. You'll find a good dry bed under the cottage.'

The Njimbin laughed hollowly and dropped the stone at once. 'Me, under there? Too busy, friend; I got plans for tonight. Just making sure my camp's safe while I'm away.' After that, of course it had to climb down and swagger off, leaving the problem of the padlock till morning. Choosing its moment it slipped into the shed and spent an uncomfortable night in a box of tools.

The bat that lived in the rafters drifted away to hunt for

moths. The Njimbin promised itself another frog-hunt in the morning. It had a new score to settle with the old woman and its anger was growing, but now it was weary and slept.

At first light it woke and went off with its dillybag for frogs. While the old woman fed the fowls it pushed its captives through the forced window-screen; they landed with resentful plops and began to search for corners in which to be alone, The Njimbin was dissatisfied, but it had not yet thought of anything better than frogs. It wandered down to the river and climbed one of the oaks in order to think.

The tide was coming in. A raft of some rubbish, or perhaps weed, drifted sluggishly with it; the Njimbin watched absently. After a time its eyes sharpened: the floating rubbish had turned out of the current and drifted near the shore.

Flotsam should not behave like that; the Njimbin stared keenly. In another moment it scuttled down from the oak and hurried to the shore.

'Ho, old friend!' it shouted. 'Got away, then, did you? And what are you after in these parts?'

The Hairy Man came heavily ashore, its rough hair sleeked by the water running off, its body like a sack and its long arms dangling below its knees.

'Frogs,' it grunted, and headed for the swamp.

The Njimbin grinned wickedly and seized what the moment had brought; for the Hairy Man was neither sly nor secretive, and the old woman would still be hobbling around with the dog.

'You won't find frogs there now,' it called cheerfully. 'Nothing but skinny little hoppers. I've got all the fat green leapers put away for you – knew you were coming – been working two days for you. Come on.'

It led the Hairy Man up the ridge to the cottage.

12

Like the Njimbin, Mrs Tucker had spent an uneasy night.
She could not lie still in bed; but neither could she turn
over, nor move a foot to rest an aching bunion, without
waiting for the tickle of ants between the sheets or the
sudden leap of a frog. When she slept, the movement of
the sheet against her chin was enough to set her
dreaming. She was glad to wake at last in daylight, and
determined that before another night came she would
somehow get rid of the pests in the cottage.

'Enough's enough,' she told Hector grimly, as she sent
him outside.

The axe and the bits of blackened wire were still on the
shelf above the stove. There was a frog on top of the
refrigerator, patiently waiting for insects. Mrs Tucker
gave it a sour look and left it alone. You couldn't spray
frogs. She needed something else: something like a
butterfly-net, maybe.

Meanwhile the fowls were waiting to be fed. Mrs
Tucker smiled grimly to find her padlock still in place
with some new scratches shining on its dullness. She took
the key from her pocket and unlocked it.

The fowls rushed at their mash in a normal way that

seemed calm and orderly. One white egg shone among the straw of the nest-box. It was a small victory and Mrs Tucker was delighted.

'There, now!' she cried, congratulating the hens. She took the warm, smooth egg into her hand. 'That's something like.'

She took Hector off for his walk feeling very much heartened, planning to send a few eggs home with young Ivan one of these days and to try a plastic bag on the end of a broom as a frog-net.

It was a sunny, busy morning after the rain. The autumn songs of magpies and butcher-birds were beginning. The small frogs down in the swamp sounded like crickets. Waves of mosquitoes came out of the grass and Mrs Tucker beat at them with a twig. The midges whirled in their soundless, slow-moving columns, so fragile they were almost invisible; Mrs Tucker suddenly thought they were like moments of time and was pleased with the idea.

She saw there was something odd about the cottage the moment she and Hector came back, for the porch door was open and only the screen-door closed. She never left the doors like that; she stopped and stiffened. She knew at once that something old and sly and tricky was now inside the cottage, for she had been expecting it ever since she had set the stone axe on the mantelshelf. Her eyes sharpened.

'Now we'll see,' she whispered to Hector.

She had no idea what she would see and disliked the thought of finding out; her legs, though stiffened, felt rubbery at the knees. But she flapped her hand forbiddingly at Hector and crept to the kitchen window. Hector grew alert and still and remembered the frogs.

Mrs Tucker cupped her hands around her eyes to cut out the sunlight and looked through the window. At first she saw only half of the kitchen, apparently empty, and her own bedroom door directly opposite. The door was partly closed, but as she looked it opened wider and a large dark figure shambled through. She could not see it clearly against her bedroom window, but it looked shaggy as if it were covered in hair. It held something in each dangling hand, something that struggled; and it was looking straight at Mrs Tucker but didn't seem to see her. As she watched, it lifted one of the struggling things, dropped it into its mouth and stood crunching. Mrs Tucker saw, by the action of one disappearing leg, that the hairy thing had eaten a frog.

If she had once imagined, in her neat room at Sunset House, that she would ever stand outside her cottage window and watch such a thing Mrs Tucker would have been shocked and shaken; she would never have left town. But at Sunset House Mrs Tucker had not been shaken by the worse fear that such a thing could not exist and that she must be going off her head. Now, as she looked, she was astonished to feel so calm. It took a little time to realize that the calm was made up of a mixture of other feelings.

Certainly she was shocked and shaken – and relieved that she saw the thing at last – astonished that it was so large and heavy and shambling – and angry and afraid. And she found that she could not stand staring at a thing that stared back without seeing, and certainly not when the thing had come shambling out of her own bedroom as if it owned the place. She was half-way to the back door before she knew she had moved.

Her knees still felt rubbery and her hand was clenched like a vice on the bent wattle stick; but her feet, acting on their own account, kept hobbling to the screen-door. Hector shouldered it open ahead of her and stood at bay in the porch, barking dangerously. The hairy thing ignored him and ate the second frog. Mrs Tucker did not like the look of that and thought that Hector was probably stupid enough to get himself hurt; also, she found that her strange false calm was too brittle to stand his barking. She grabbed Hector's collar, levered at him with her stick, managed to get him outside and shut the door. Hector went on barking – from the back door, the side window, the front verandah. Evidently he was rushing round the house.

Mrs Tucker turned back and faced the hairy thing. 'And what do you think *you're* doing?' she demanded.

It looked at her. Its eyes were dark and heavily browed. It did not look old but its eyes were as old as a lizard's. Mrs Tucker's old-blue eyes gazed back. Something – a sense of pity or of fellowship – flowed between them. Then the hairy thing put out a long arm and brushed her aside. She fell into a chair while the long arm shot past her and seized the frog from the top of the refrigerator.

After that the hairy thing prowled along the base of the kitchen walls and prodded into corners and jerked cupboards open. It recovered three frogs, one from the corner under the stove and two from under the kitchen sink, and held them bunched by the back legs in a jerking, squarking bouquet. Mrs Tucker stayed where she was on the kitchen chair; she had a passing thought that the hairy thing was doing a better job than she and Hector could do, but mainly she was puzzled.

She remembered the stone axe and glanced quickly up at the mantelshelf. There was a movement just as quick something like a shadow that slipped down behind the refrigerator – and Mrs Tucker's mind cried *Ahah!* For in that fraction of a second, that slipping of a shadow, there had been a glimpse of a gnarled old face, sly old eyes, and a tricky wicked grin. And Mrs Tucker knew that now, truly, she had seen her enemy.

The frog-eating thing was now slouching off to the front rooms, and she watched it go with something like scorn. Of course it couldn't be the one that lived in the fowlhouse. Too heavy and slow, for one thing. Too big, too easily seen. And not enough mischief. Hector knew it too; he had not been angry as the enemy made him angry. So the hairy thing was new, an outsider – but not, she knew, an accident. It was one of the tricks of that swift and sly old thing that was now behind the refrigerator.

From the front rooms came the bump and scrape of boxes and old furniture being pushed around. The back door thudded as Hector hurled himself against it yelling threats. Mrs Tucker laughed suddenly and spoke to the refrigerator.

'Fancy trying to scare me with a thing like that at my age! It seems I know you better than you know me. Now you've got your axe,' for she knew without properly looking that it was gone, 'you'd better clear off, and take your frogs and your hairy friend with you. If you come back here I might turn the key on you and have a good look at you.'

She stood up, walked carefully into her bedroom and shut the door. Then she lay on her bed and listened to the bumping and scraping, the slamming of doors, the excited barking that rose at last to real anger, until finally the house was quiet. She felt like someone on the shore watching an action at sea; but she found that she was shivering and pulled the knitted rug around her till she was warm again.

Later she got up and called Hector inside. She gave him a biscuit and a gentle battering to make up for having shut him out when he was in the right of it. After that she sat in the kitchen and drank a cup of tea.

The axe was gone, sure enough, and the bits of wire with it. There was nothing left that she could show to anyone else; she was on her own again. She felt tired, limp and proud, for now she was certain she could stand up to the worst that the old mischief could do.

13

That afternoon – while the blue haze deepened on the hills, and the gentle autumn sun sparkled on the Broad, and tiny new pines reached for it in the forests of grass – Mrs Tucker stayed indoors. She began another letter to her daughter Helen, giving as usual the address of her old friend Doris. She felt secure indoors, for with Hector as peaceful as a lizard on a log she knew there could be no old things here, sly or hairy.

But a dog can't stay in all the time and the fowls would be wanting their wheat; it was funny how fast that bag had gone down. In the late afternoon Mrs Tucker took another can of wheat from it and ventured out; but this time she locked the cottage doors, and took with her the keys on the wire ring that the solicitor had given her.

She had been thinking, between the careful sentences of her letter, about the padlock on the fowlhouse door. It was, like other victories, more worry than it was worth. If she left it there the old thing would be spiteful; if she took it off the fowls would get fidgety again. At last she had decided to take it off as a peace-making gesture, in the hope that the old thing would be pleased and would give up making the fowls fidgety.

It was too late, she found. The wire netting of the fowlrun now sagged untidily from a post where two of her nails had been forced. There was a gap a foot wide near the top of the fence, and the fowls were rushing nervously about the yard.

'Tchut!' spat Mrs Tucker. She was vexed and upset. Now she had lost both her victory and her peace-making gesture, and tomorrow she would have to mend the fence again. She took the padlock away with a very bad grace.

By next day, when she mended the fence, the fowls seemed hungry again. It also happened that she hefted the bag of wheat that had gone down so fast and discovered both the rats' arrangements for their own supply and the bricks that had cut it off. Mrs Tucker's moustache bristled. She was providing for more than fowls, by the look of it.

'I'm fed up with it,' she declared to Hector. He could see that this was true, and crept off to his basket with ears and tail folded down in case he should do or say something to make matters worse.

Mrs Tucker waited for young Ivan to come putt-putting up the track, and asked him if his mother kept fowls.

Young Ivan nodded.

'Would she take mine off my hands? I can't be bothered with the fidgety things. Something's upsetting them and it's more than rats. I've only had the one egg and I've made up my mind: they won't settle without they have company.'

Young Ivan looked stern and marched off to inspect the fowlrun. There were no new rat-holes and everything looked tight and trim. Young Ivan spoke a word: 'Foxes.'

94

He thought for a moment and added another: 'Goannas.'
Then he turned his brother's motorcycle and went
sputtering off.

Mrs Tucker thought he had gone to consult his
mother, but in a little while she heard him sputtering
back. He had brought his brother's rifle and a pocketful
of stolen cartridges.

'Snakes alive!' bellowed Mrs Tucker. 'What are you
going to do with that?' She seized Hector by the collar
and dragged him inside.

Young Ivan, sternly frowning, stalked off with the rifle.
Soon Mrs Tucker began to hear the flat *crack* of shots from
up and down the ridge and on the flats. It was impossible
that young Ivan could have found so many foxes and
goannas conveniently at hand. She could only guess that
he meant to alarm and unsettle any that might be within
hearing, persuading them to move to other parts. He
came back at last, carrying a dead hare by the ears and
looking self-satisfied, nodded to Mrs Tucker in con-
gratulation, mounted the cycle with some difficulty and
rode away. Mrs Tucker hissed and tutted and muttered.
She would have to try again to get rid of her fowls.

The Njimbin and the Hairy Man were down on the
flats when the shooting began. The Hairy Man was
poking into pools and prodding under logs in search of
frogs. The Njimbin, no longer friendly, was trying to
persuade it to go away.

'You've had frogs,' it said reasonably. 'Cleaned 'em
out. What more do you want?'

'More frogs,' grunted the Hairy Man.

'There *are* no more. You've had all the big ones and
most of the little hoppers too. Better try somewhere else.'

95

The Hairy Man, slumped beside a pool, turned its dark, disgruntled eyes on the Njimbin. 'So many frogs we keep stepping on 'em,' it taunted. 'Lotta jabber-jabber. Mighta known. Like that dog.'

The Njimbin glowered, but it would do no good to quarrel with the Hairy Man; it put on an injured tone. 'We had the frogs. Only I forgot how fast you eat. Now I've got all these ibis going hungry, and the hawks and snakes – what am I going to tell 'em, eh? I met an old friend and gave away all their tucker out of the goodness of my heart? I'll get no more thanks from them than I get from you.'

The Hairy Man only shrugged. The Njimbin looked exasperated, but before it could speak again there came the crack of the rifle and an angry little *zt* from the swampy ground at its feet. The Njimbin darted behind an oak. The Hairy Man turned its dark old eyes to the ridge where young Ivan stood with the rifle.

Neither creature knew what would happen if it were struck by a bullet. Death was rare among their kind and none had ever been shot – but this might be because their kind was swift to avoid trouble. They knew what could happen to a bird or a wallaby and preferred to leave it at that. The Hairy Man loped a few yards to the riverbank and slid into the water. Soon it had become a raft of weed or rubbish drifting away on the tide.

This pleased the Njimbin so much that it enjoyed dodging young Ivan's bullets. It knew the boy, had often seen him bring food to the old woman, and believed she had sent him now. It jeered in triumph as it slipped from shelter to shelter.

After the boy had ridden away the Njimbin danced a

short victory-dance. Then it went to find its waddy, for it fancied a dinner of young and innocent rat. It had a tinful of wheat and mash stolen from the fowl's feedings, and it knew that by now the rats would be eager for the treat. Hadn't it cut off their private supply and then left them to forage for themselves, on purpose to teach them a lesson? In fact the Njimbin was full of self-satisfaction: it had brought the rats to heel, taught the old woman the futility of padlocks and rifles, and got rid of the Hairy Man. It swaggered off to the wombat burrow that it used as a store.

The weapons lay together within reach of a Njimbin's arm. As it drew them out it felt at once that something was wrong; the weight or the balance was not right. The Njimbin's eyes hardened. It laid the weapons on the grass: the waddy, the axe and the spear. But the spear was broken.

Young Ivan had fired a shot into the burrow, just in case. The head of the spear was shattered and splintered: the Njimbin did not need to know how. It knew well enough who was to blame.

It had been angry about the traps and the padlock, but a Njimbin who camped in a fowlrun must expect to deal with troubles of that kind. It had been angry about the axe, but that had been a misfortune of war; the Njimbin itself had dropped the axe into the old woman's hands. This was a different matter: war brought into its own territory; its secret store invaded, a good spear smashed and defiantly left for the Njimbin to find. This time the old thing did not sulk or rage or invent small revenges. It replaced the weapons and stood erect: gnarled and ancient, a small angry power of the land.

It happened that at that moment Mrs Tucker switched on her kitchen light. The cottage windows glowed dim and yellow in the twilight. The Njimbin fixed its eyes on the glow, but it did not see the cottage itself, or the fowlrun, or the shabby straggling scrub. It saw that yellow glow within forests remote and grand and filled with life; the great boughs lifting fragile orchids to the sun, the great trunks feathered with fern, the great roots bedded in moss; the leaves falling and rotting where the seeds lay. It saw the flashing of bird-wings, the darting of lizards, the busy roads of ants and beetles; the old patterns, the old blind brotherhoods, that by their power sustained and supported the forest. And the Njimbin called again on the power of little things.

'Come,' it commanded silently. And they came.

14

Mrs Tucker, scrambling eggs for her dinner, was still frowning and tutting over young Ivan's gun-battle with the forces of nature. She had passed the point of grumbling things like 'The boy meant no harm' and 'No use crying over spilt milk' and 'Least said soonest mended'. She had now reached the point of explaining forcibly to Hector the harm that might have happened and the things that ought to be said.

'And what if you'd been out there in the blady-grass?' she argued, pointing her wooden spoon at him. 'You might've been shot!'

Hector beat his tail soothingly on the floor, reminding her that she had taken care of that by dragging him inside by the neck.

'And what about someone fishing?' she retorted, picking a fallen midge out of the egg. 'Or a stray dog? Or a horse?'

Hector's peaceable tail suggested that young Ivan would probably have noticed a horse.

'The idea!' rumbled Mrs Tucker, scraping egg on to a plate after blowing several midges off. 'Letting a child that age run loose with a rifle.' Anticipating Hector's comment that Ivan's family probably didn't know, she added, 'Rifles and cartridges ought to be kept locked up, anyone knows that.' Hector agreed, so she sat down at the table with a bump.

She took up her fork. Light and inconsequential, three dead midges drifted on to her plate. Mrs Tucker glanced at the light above the table, muttered *tchut*, and removed her chair and her plate to the corner near the stove. She left her plate on the edge of the stove while she went through the cottage and closed all the windows.

'Rain's gone,' she explained to Hector. 'They'll all be out tonight.'

She ate her scrambled eggs while the midges wove a delicate whirling net around the electric bulb, then lightly and mysteriously died, and drifted down to lie invisible on the brown table. They were so weightless and soundless, so gentle and harmless, it was hard to remember they were there at all; but Mrs Tucker's neck and her white hair felt tiny messages of movement. She humped her shoulders, batted at her topknot crossly and glanced up again. The upper air of the kitchen, between hanging bulb and ceiling, was alive with midges.

'My sainted aunt!' boomed Mrs Tucker, and reached for the spray-can.

Caught in the jet of spray, the tiny helpless things whirled and streamed and obediently died. Lighter than dust they filtered slowly down to sprinkle the flat surfaces of the room. Mrs Tucker had to bring her dustpan and brush, and then her broom, to sweep them up. Her own nose tingled from the spray, but by the time she had finished, the upper air was alive as before and a new net whirled about the light. Since she had already shut the windows there was nothing else she could do.

'Maggoty things,' she muttered – and suddenly stopped to listen. Somewhere there was a sound: not here where the midges drifted and settled and crawled, but somewhere out in the night. Mrs Tucker put down her dustpan and went to the window. With her face against the glass she looked along the broad beam of light that flowed out from the kitchen.

It fell on something grey, only feet from the wall – something that filled the patch of light and loomed beyond – a great dark mass that cut off the northern stars. At first she thought this thing was solid, but then she saw it was packed with swirling movement; and out of it came a strange high note of singing, gentle as a cradle-song but filling all the night. Mrs Tucker's old mind fumbled. She looked and shivered.

Then she saw that the screen outside the window was moving too, and then the glass itself, and a depth of grey shadow lay on the sill. She thought the vast, singing mass that swirled outside the cottage was dissolving it before her eyes, and she was afraid. At last she saw that what moved on the screen and the glass was a film of crawling midges – but what the grey moving mass beyond might be she could not believe.

And her scalp and neck tickled with thistledown crawling.

She made herself leave the window, took her flashlight to the dark front windows and probed through them with its beam. The grey swirling mass closed all round the cottage, swallowing it; and the voices of all the midges, each too fine to be heard on its own, sang together that one gentle note that filled the night. It was this she believed at last, for she remembered almost hearing that high, fine note on her pillow one night.

She could feel the persistent, harmless, thistledown crawling here in the dark as she had in the lighted kitchen; her skin tingled with it. She did not know how to shelter from this vast, relentless storm of midges. She stumbled through the cottage stuffing paper and clothing under doors and round window-frames, brushing midges from her lips, wiping them from stinging eyes, rubbing them from her nose. Afterwards she went through the rooms with the spray-can. It was empty before she had finished but she went on spraying, for she knew despairingly that it made no difference; nothing made a difference. She could not cover all the gaps between boards, all the invisible chinks that the ants came through; she could not keep the little, inoffensive creatures out. And the night was still filled with that soft, immense note of singing.

In every room, as she switched on the light, a grey mist drifted down from the ceiling to swirl around the bulb. Caught in the spray they died lightly and readily; she thought it did not matter much to them. They were momentary things. They died as lightly in their dances round the bulbs, and outside the windows the grey fluff of their dead lay deep on every sill. It did not matter to them. The living seeped in to replace the dead, and the midge-voice sang from the grey whirling mass that her flashlight-beam could not penetrate. She dropped the empty spray-can and stood helpless.

Hector had crept into the dark patch under the kitchen table. There he sat patient and enduring, but jerkily scratching from time to time. Mrs Tucker got laboriously down to the floor and crawled in with him; the table was a little shelter. She knew she should put out the kitchen light, that it shone enticingly from ridge to ridge, but it was a hard thing to do. It would not remove the hordes that were already inside and she thought, as she slapped at her ears and brushed at her face and neck, that in the dark she could not endure their relentless, weightless crawling.

But the air thickened; no matter how she coughed and snorted there were midges in Mrs Tucker's nose and mouth and throat. She thought with horror of suffocating, her lungs full of winged grey fluff. Hector had buried his nose in the soft fur of his flank: Mrs Tucker hauled herself up on a chair and went to her bedroom for one of John Bright's big handkerchiefs. She tied it as a mask over her nose and mouth, switched off the light, and fumbled her way back under the table. She sat with Hector in the dark and waited for this gentle, tormenting, suffocating, soft-singing storm to pass.

It did not pass. The white walls of the cottage gleamed in the dark, and the Njimbin sat on the roof and called, 'Come.'

In the kitchen the air cleared as the midges settled, and now the table was no shelter from them. They crawled endlessly, relentlessly: into Hector's white fur and Mrs Tucker's white hair; over and under her white mask; into her ears and inside her clothes. She stayed where she was because Hector did and endured as he did, forced into patience but slapping and twitching, while her mind gathered thoughts and prodded at them. Sometimes she shared them with Hector: once she said, 'No good ever comes of playing with rifles', and another time, 'One for every soul that ever breathed. And there's nothing you can do.' Some time later she said passionately, 'Why don't you *talk?*' and Hector licked her hand in the dark. He knew the question was not illogical or pointless.

In another hour Mrs Tucker had made up her mind. She said tiredly, 'That's enough then. Whatever else we're made to do, we won't be made to sleep under a table.' And she crawled out and pulled herself up on a chair. Groping in the dark, she put Hector to bed in his basket. She stripped the white linen from her bed and laid it on the table. Then she put cottonwool in her ears and lay down on her bed, covering herself from head to foot with the knitted patchwork rug. In time she even slept.

Towards midnight a breeze came up and blew the midge-storm away.

It left the devastation of a storm. Mrs Tucker found it in the morning. Trapped between every window and its screen the winged grey fluff of dead midges lay four inches deep; if she opened the windows every breeze would carry the light-flying stuff through the house. The front verandah was deeply carpeted in it; she could not walk there. Within the cottage every flat surface – floors, chair-seats, tables, benches; the tops of cupboards and the refrigerator; the kitchen sink and the dinner-plate still unwashed – was misted and littered with grey. Some of this mist was still living and crawled away from a broom. Some of it was dead and blew away at a breath – but swept away it left grey streaks to be washed off. It was more work than repairing a fowlrun and too much for one old woman.

Mrs Tucker fed her fowls. The autumn spider-webs were not silver but grey, and the cottage was hung with grey cobwebs she had not known were there. She took Hector walking. In every shade the midges, as frail as moments of time, built their shimmering, threatening columns. She sat on a log and gazed over the sunlit water. There, lower down the ridge, was her cottage, alone in a landscape swarming with unseen life, its tired old frame vulnerable to rats and frogs and snakes and midges and fire.

She went over the thinking she had done last night. She did not know about the rats, who accepted the Njimbin's care and paid the price of it. She did know she had been given the same kind of choice; and she was old and alone and knew reality. She could battle with one small old magic for the use of her fowlhouse, but Ivan and his gun had widened the battle into a war. She had always known that the old thing was part of the land itself, and she could not fight a war against the land. Hector gave up whuffling through the grass and sat near, till at last Mrs Tucker took up her bent stick and hobbled home.

After breakfast she began on the cleaning. She cleaned one or two window-sills so that she could open the windows, and swept the verandah so that she could open the front door. Then she sat down and drank a cup of tea. Afterwards she blew and dusted a few surfaces so that she could cook and wash. By then she was tired and fidgety and there was still a lot to do.

'It'll have to wait,' she grumbled.

In the afternoon she tore up the letter she had written to her daughter Helen and began another, and this time she put her own address at the top.

'You might as well know where I am,' she wrote, 'in case of accidents.' And she told about the cottage, and the boat, and Hector; about young Ivan and the groceries and the rifle; about the fowls that were unsettled, perhaps by a tramp; about the rain bringing the ants inside, but no flood this time; and how the grass had grown so high you could hardly walk, but as for snakes she had her gumboots. It was a long letter. It finished, 'I am well and happy as I hope you are, so no need to worry. Give my love to little Valerie.'

Mrs Tucker sealed the letter and put it on the shelf above the stove to wait for young Ivan's next visit. If she had been younger she would have wept.

15

'How could you, Mother?' wailed Helen, standing in Mrs Tucker's kitchen and still clutching her smart black handbag. 'After we'd been through all the business of Sunset House, and everything there so nice – coming to a place like this and not a word to anyone. I don't understand how you could!'

'Now that's enough, Helen,' Mrs Tucker boomed, for she had a sore conscience on that point and there were real tears in Helen's eyes. 'You fetch me another cup from that cupboard and sit down and drink your tea. You always were too highly strung. When we took the room at Sunset House I didn't know I had a cottage of my own, did I?'

'And never telling a word about it,' Helen moaned; but she saw Mrs Tucker's moustache bristle, so dabbed her eyes and turned obediently to the cupboard. She fiddled with the cups in an embarrassed way. 'There seem to be . . . some dead insects . . . .'

Mrs Tucker laughed. She was still cleaning up at her own pace, but Helen had come so quickly that there hadn't been time to do it all.

She said, 'More than a few or I'm a Dutchman. Midges.

They're into everything. They won't hurt you, just blow them off.' And she thought that if only she'd been able to say that on the night of the midge-storm, to someone like poor Helen, maybe the old thing in the fowlhouse wouldn't have beaten her. She took the cup that Helen reluctantly passed and began to pour tea.

'I've been sick with worry,' said Helen reproachfully, 'thinking of you here, alone at your age, miles away from us all. With floods and bushfires and snakes – you must come back, Mother. It wouldn't be fair – I couldn't sleep at night.'

'My stars,' said Mrs Tucker, passing tea and sitting down, 'I've been having the time of my life. It suits me better than one room with a lot of old biddies all round; and John lived here till the day he died. Would he leave it to me if he thought I couldn't live in it?'

'But Mother! Of course Uncle John didn't mean you to live in it! Alone at your age, with floods and bush-fires . . . .'

'Rubbish, Helen. What else would John mean?'

'He meant you to sell it, of course!' cried Helen. 'To have the money to be comfortable. Buy a little place near your family; something like that.'

Mrs Tucker looked down at the table in case Helen should catch the gleam in her eyes; it was going very nicely. She said thoughtfully, 'You mean in town? A little place with a yard for Hector and a bit of garden? With a good paling fence between me and the neighbours?'

'Of course . . . if you think you can manage for yourself . . . if it's what you want . . . .'

'It might do at a pinch. If this place would fetch the money. But I'm too old to go through all that business of prices for this and that, and buying and selling . . . .'

'But we'd look after that for you, Mother! We'd like to. I'll see the estate agent on my way home.'

'Don't rush me, child,' said Mrs Tucker. 'You must give me time to think. I've been very happy here, you know. But of course I don't want to worry anyone. We'll see.'

Later, when Helen had gone, she went restlessly through her cottage cleaning up a few more midges and sighing from time to time. This cottage had given her back a great deal: the dignity of independence in her own home; the right to risk breaking her leg in a fall from a stepladder; the freedom to choose her own undershirts and her own company.

'Though the dear knows how you'll get on in town,' she said to Hector. Still, she knew he had sense, and in any case that was another question; another problem still to come, life to be lived in your own way without other people doing it for you. John and his cottage had saved her from Sunset House.

And Helen, properly managed, had saved her too: from the lonely chill of a place that didn't know her or want her, and from all the little, terrible things that swarmed in it. She knew she ought to be pleased and excited, proud to have managed the whole thing from start to finish, eager to discover and buy her next home. In a little while, perhaps, she would be excited; there were weeks of waiting and planning still to come. Now she felt only restless and cross and dissatisfied.

'Old mischief,' she muttered to herself. Not even to Hector would she confess how she hated to go meekly back to town and leave the land's old thing victorious in her fowlhouse.

109

She pulled open cupboards and drawers, frowning at all John's stuff that would have to be sorted, and shook her head at the old newspapers in the front room. 'They'll want it all clean and clear before they sell,' she grumbled at Hector. 'There'll have to be a bonfire. Helen can see to it.'

Hector gave a soothing tail-wag and followed her out to the shed, where she prodded at things and turned them over and grew more belligerent. 'I'll take what I want, any road, and never mind the carrier. The rest can burn.'

She shoved pliers and screwdrivers into a box of old hinges and door-handles, added a tin of nails and a bundle of washers. The little hand-saw cheered her; she put it aside with the box, a hammer, and the stepladder – and suddenly straightened, looking down at Hector.

'A bonfire,' she muttered, with a glint in her old-blue eyes; and then, 'Not yet – we don't want more midges, or snakes or worse. A bonfire the day we go, and young Ivan can keep an eye on it after.'

Briskly she began to drag things out from corners and under the bench: a box of oily rags, some offcuts of timber, the bottle of linseed oil with the leaky cork. These and more she carried over to the fowlhouse and stacked against its wall, but she did not speak again though Hector followed her anxiously back and forth. He only saw that her eyes were still glinting and her moustache bristled. She said nothing until he had followed her back into the kitchen, where she dropped into a chair and reached down to batter his ears.

'Maggoty old fowlhouse,' she whispered happily. 'John should've put a match to it long ago if he'd known. Mum's the word, mind. Walls have ears.' She gave a

110

sudden bellow of laughter. 'We'll go out with a bang, any road. I'd like to see that old thing's face.' Hector gave her a reproachful look and flopped down heavily on the doormat.

'That's right,' said Mrs Tucker 'Enough's enough for today. You take the weight off your feet, and later on we'll go down and have a look at the boat.'

Hector gave a deep and dismal sigh.